Dark Origin

DCI Dani Bevan #9

By

KATHERINE
PATHAK

THE GARANSAY PRESS

2

Books by Katherine Pathak

The Imogen and Hugh Croft Mysteries:

Aoife's Chariot

The Only Survivor

Lawful Death

The Woman Who Vanished

Memorial for the Dead
(Introducing DCI Dani Bevan)

The Ghost of Marchmont Hall

Short Story collection:

The Flawed Emerald and other Stories

DCI Dani Bevan novels:

Against A Dark Sky

On A Dark Sea

A Dark Shadow Falls

Dark as Night

The Dark Fear

Girls of The Dark

Hold Hands in the Dark

Dark Remedies

Dark Origin

Standalone novels:

I Trust You

4

#DarkOrigin

Edited by: The Currie Revisionists, 2017

© Cover photograph Pixabay Images

PROLOGUE

AN adolescent boy sat hunch-shouldered in the waiting area outside Gordon Lafferty's office. The boy was lanky and heavy-boned, a mop of blondish hair hanging low over his sulky features.

A couple in their mid-forties, smartly dressed and harassed-looking, burst through the doors to the school's reception. The boy's rounded shoulders flinched ever so slightly at the sound of their arrival.

"We're here to see Mr Lafferty," the woman said breathlessly. "Something to do with an incident on the games field?"

The secretary glanced up from her keyboard. "Hal is sitting over there, Mrs Gill. Perhaps you'd like to take a seat with your son until the headmaster is ready?"

Mr Gill puffed out his chest. "Will this take long? I had to leave a very important meeting. I was under the impression someone had been injured. Hal looks perfectly okay to me."

The secretary removed her glasses and observed the man carefully. For the first time, the couple could see that the woman's eyes were puffy and a little blood-shot, as if she'd been crying. "It wasn't Hal who was injured, Mr and Mrs Gill. *Now*, if you could *please* take a chair next to you son, Mr Lafferty will be out to speak with you when he is good and ready. Not a minute before."

Recognising when they had been chastised, the couple moved silently across the foyer to join the boy, who had kept his head hanging down throughout this exchange, as if closely examining the condition of his shoes.

Mrs Gill placed her hand on his shoulder. "Hal,

are you okay? Can you tell us what happened before we go in? It might help if we have the facts straight. Then we can defend you to the headmaster."

The boy tilted his head to the side, so that he could eye his mother through a thick curtain of greasy fringe. "You'll have trouble this time, Sarah, dear."

His father sighed. "Show a bit more respect, will you? We've dropped everything to get here. The least you can do is enlighten us as to your latest misdemeanour."

The secretary cleared her throat, in a way that sounded as if she might be resisting an urge to make a point.

Hal fixed his father with a cold stare. "I'm afraid this little transgression might not be quite so easy for you to gloss over." He sat up straighter and brushed imaginary fluff from his uniform trousers. "I've killed someone."

The statement was made so matter-of-factly and with such a lack of emotion that Mr Gill automatically shook his head, as if to dismiss it outright as nonsense.

But Sarah Gill has seen the darkness in her son's eyes as he spoke the words. She immediately leapt to her feet, the plastic chair tipping to the floor behind her with a pitiful clatter. Then she gazed up at the ceiling and screamed. The terrible noise of her wails didn't stop until Mr Gill caught hold of her roughly and slapped her hard across the face.

Chapter 1

DCS Ronnie Douglas was pacing back and forth across his office. His tall frame meant he could cover the meagre length in just a couple of strides.

DCI Dani Bevan was beginning to find the action hypnotic. "I need a DI in my department, Sir. I will definitely be putting in a request for Alice Mann to remain in the serious crime unit. She's an excellent officer."

"I agree, but Glasgow aren't the only division out there. I know that City and Borders are seriously short-handed right now. I believe our new Detective Inspector will have her pick of posts. She's no ties to keep her here, has she?"

Dani shook her head. "No, she doesn't. Alice is in a flat share, so there isn't even a property to worry about." She sighed. "We'll just have to hope that the latitude I've given her on recent cases will persuade Alice that she will learn more if she stays put."

Douglas finally stood still. "If the girl is sensible, she will. Alice will be given a far longer leash if she serves under a female senior officer." He waggled his finger at Dani. "Don't let on I said that. I spend half my life telling committees and journalists how egalitarian we have become as an institution. But I know what male officers can be like. You can't change human nature – not in just a handful of years, anyhow."

Dani nodded, surprised at her boss's insight. She couldn't agree more. "I'll do my best to keep her on board, Sir."

"Good," Douglas grunted, before sliding behind his desk and powering up the screen of his computer, an indication that the DCI was now dismissed.

*

Ds Andy Calder was tapping feverishly at his computer keyboard as Bevan passed his desk. The man glanced up momentarily from his labours. "Morning, Ma'am."

"Is that the Dalgleish file, Andy?" She commented amiably.

"Aye, the Fiscal's office want it by noon. The case goes to court on Wednesday." His eyes had already switched back to the screen.

"I'll leave you to it, then." Dani continued to her small corner office, closing the door behind her.

Len Dalgleish was an unassuming 54 year-old bank clerk from Newton Mearns. Calder and Mann had clocked him kerb crawling on Paisley Street at two in the morning. Dalgleish had brazenly hung out of his car window and propositioned a woman right in front of them. The officers were on another job at the time so they noted his registration and chased it up a couple of days later.

They'd clearly taken Dalgleish by surprise turning up at his three-bed semi in the south west suburb at half past four on a Saturday afternoon. Alice peered through the living room window, where despite the fact a tatty venetian blind had been lowered, it was still possible to identify, through the bent and broken slats, a macabre scene of hardcore porn being acted out for the benefit of a large, professional-looking camera standing in one corner, where the telly should have been.

Assessing that there may have been a risk of violence to the participants, a couple of whom appeared to be minors, Andy kicked the front door in.

Calder apprehended Dalgleish, who was acting as a kind of sleazy film director, whilst Alice Mann took down the details of the girls, most of them naked or only partially dressed, before calling the station for immediate back-up.

Evidence found at the property revealed Leonard Dalgleish was a prolific producer of particularly nasty online pornography. A few of the girls they managed to identify from the films were as young as 13. The case was immediately passed on to Vice, but Dani's division were required to assist with the assiduous process of evidence collection. Calder in particular, was keen to ensure the Fiscal's case against the man was watertight.

Dani was just thanking her lucky stars that her officers hadn't needed to view the hours upon hours of deeply unpleasant digital recordings, when a call came through to her desk.

"I've got a Fergus Kelso on the line for you, Ma'am. He says you know him."

Dani was surprised to hear the name of the Edinburgh lawyer who had worked on the Nancy Duff death row appeal. "Sure, put him through."

"DCI Bevan, I'm sorry to intrude on your working day like this."

"What can I do for you, Mr Kelso?" Dani recalled the young man's head of full, dark hair and his charming manner.

He sighed on the other end of the line. "For the past two months, I've been assisting with another death sentence appeal. This case is quite different to the one in Virginia. I need some insight from a police officer to help me make sense of the evidence." Kelso cleared his throat awkwardly. "But more than that, I would really appreciate a *female* perspective on the situation. I know it sounds odd, but when you hear the details, I think you'd understand."

Dani could tell the lawyer was on tenterhooks, clearly concerned the DCI would take offence at the request. She didn't at all. "Look, Mr Kelso, I really can't spare you any time right now. You can imagine how busy the division are." She could sense his disappointment, the emotion almost crackled across the line. "But I do know a person who might just be able to provide the insight you need."

Chapter 2

Alice was secretly relieved to have been temporarily taken off the Dalgleish case. She knew that Calder was keen to follow the investigation through to its conclusion, but Vice had never been an area of detection that interested her much.

She was also aware that Calder's sense of outrage at the exploitation of the young and vulnerable was what drove him to want to nail nasty perps like Dalgleish. Alice felt that way too. But the collating of pornographic material and the laborious cross-checking of the databases they had for women arrested for prostitution or in raids on brothels across the city just didn't stimulate her. There wasn't enough of a puzzle to solve.

So, Alice was intrigued when the DCI asked if she'd be interested in having a couple of days away from the division to liaise with a prominent human rights lawyer in Edinburgh. In fact, she'd jumped at the chance, thinking it would give her an opportunity to check out the vibe of the city. Decide if maybe this was a good place to take up her post as DI.

It wasn't perhaps the best day for it. The grey clouds were hanging low over Auld Reekie and a smir of drizzle was making the atmosphere cold and dank. Alice arrived at a busy café on Duncan Street and managed to find a table for two across from the counter. She'd just ordered a coffee when a well-dressed man pushed through the entrance door.

Alice knew immediately this was the lawyer she'd arranged to meet.

Fergus Kelso was clearly a regular. He made a well-practised gesture to a young barista before lowering himself onto the seat opposite Alice.

The detective put out her hand. "DI Alice Mann. Although, you didn't seem to have a problem identifying me." She smiled wryly.

Kelso smiled back. "I come in here every day for my regular caffeine hit. I know my fellow addicts pretty well."

"Your office must be nearby then?"

"Yes, the chambers are a couple of streets away." He paused as the barista set down Alice's cup of flat white and Kelso's tiny double espresso. "Although I'm hardly there much. My work takes me all over the world."

Alice recognised this comment as the introduction to the topic Kelso was here to discuss. "DCI Bevan said you wanted a cop's perspective on your current case?"

The man nodded, looking a little uncomfortable. "Obviously, I have several contacts on the police force here at City and Borders, but I met your boss last year in the States. I felt like she had a particular insight that, if I'm honest, I wished to take advantage of."

Alice chuckled. "I apologise for being sloppy seconds. I've worked with Bevan on a number of cases. I'm not suggesting it's the same thing, but I can give you the benefit of my humble opinion."

Kelso caught her eye, his expression penitent. "I didn't mean to imply you were second best. If Bevan recommended you, I have every faith you will be her equal."

Something about the earnestness of the man's words made a flush creep up Alice's pale cheeks, a characteristic that had plagued the detective since childhood. Her mother said it went hand-in-hand with the auburn hair and healthy sprinkling of freckles. She took a long sip of coffee, in an attempt to mask her discomfort. "Great, tell me more then."

Kelso sat back in his seat, running a hand through his thick hair, left longer on top to accentuate a natural kink. "It's not the kind of case I usually take on. My client is on death row in China. To be honest, the process is usually shrouded in mystery. The authorities treat all capital cases as state secrets. Despite the fact China executes more people each year than any other country - according to Amnesty International figures - we hear very little about it."

Alice shrugged her shoulders. "I don't know anything about the Chinese justice system."

"Very few folk do, including the Chinese themselves. Charmian Zhu, née Wilson, is forty-nine years old and has dual nationality. She was born in Pitlochry and lived there with her parents until going up to Oxford. She gained a first-class honours degree in Economics from St Margaret's College, Oxford in 1989. She got a job with an international bank and moved out to Hong Kong after graduation."

"She was living there when Hong Kong was transferred back from the British to the Chinese government?"

Kelso nodded, impressed by her general knowledge. "That's right. After '91 a lot of British ex-pats in Hong Kong returned home. But Charmian had met her future husband by then. Zhu Deming was ten years her senior and a big wheel at one of China's premier trust management companies. They married in '92 and subsequently moved to Beijing, where Deming's family originated from."

"Mrs Zhu hasn't lived in the UK for twenty-seven

years?" Alice raised her eyebrows.

"That's right. Although she travelled back often enough to visit her parents and for business. The last time she was in Scotland was the summer of 2013."

"And now she's in a Chinese jail?"

A look of sadness passed across Kelso's features. "I visited her last month at the facility outside Beijing where she is being held. Charmian was once a great beauty. I've seen the photos. Now she's shockingly thin and her skin is terribly aged. She's like a different person."

"What happened to put her there?" Alice was determined to hear the facts and not be swayed by sentimentality.

"Charmian and her Chinese husband appeared to have a good marriage. There were no children, but both had busy and successful careers. They holidayed regularly and in exotic locations. I've spoken with several of their friends who confirmed a happy relationship. Then, in September of last year, a few days after the couple had returned from one of their overseas trips, residents of their apartment block in downtown Beijing reported a noisy disturbance to the security manager." Kelso fiddled with a sugar sachet on the table between them. "He took the elevator to the Zhus' floor and knocked repeatedly at the door. The manager could hear movement inside but no one was opening up. After five minutes of hammering, he unlocked the door with his pass."

"What did he find?"

"Zhu Deming was lying on the floor of the living room with a bullet wound to the side of his temple. The gun was positioned on a rug a few feet away."

"And Charmian?"

"The manager found her in the bedroom. She was

wearing a towelling robe and her hair was wet, as if she'd just got out of the shower. Charmian was cowering between the bed and the window, with her hands over her face."

"Was she in shock?"

"I assume so. The manager asked if she was okay. He didn't get much of a response so he rushed back out to Deming. It was glaringly obvious the man was dead. I've looked at the scene of crime photos. The pool of blood almost filled the floor. The manager had no choice but to call the police. The medics showed up too, but their presence was a formality."

Alice shuddered. "Any signs of a break-in? What floor was the apartment on?"

Kelso cleared his throat a little awkwardly. "The tenth floor. They were roughly a hundred and fifty feet from street level."

"*Okay*, so what about an exterior fire escape, or balconies?"

"There was no exterior fire escape, just an interior stairwell in addition to the elevator. But each flat possessed a narrow balcony protruding from the lounge area, beyond sliding glass doors. In the case of the Zhu residence, the doors were found to be locked on the evening Deming was killed. The keys were kept in one of the kitchen cupboards."

Alice finished her coffee. "Sounds like an inside job. What about gun residue on Charmian's hands and clothing? I'm assuming she was the chief suspect from the start?"

"Charmian claimed she discovered her husband dead *after* her shower. She maintains he must have taken his own life while she was out of the room. Charmian stepped out of the shower cubicle, dried herself and went into the lounge to get her hairdryer from one of the cases still out in the hallway. They'd not yet properly unpacked. She found Deming on the floor, the gun a few inches from his right hand. As she dropped down beside him to see if he was alive, she moved the gun to one side."

Alice crinkled her face with obvious scepticism. "Was it Deming's gun?"

"It was Charmian's. She kept it in the apartment for when her husband was away on business. It made her feel safer." Kelso saw Alice's expression grow incredulous, so he ploughed on, "but no residue was found on Charmian's skin or robe. There were fingerprints on the gun, of course; fresh and historic. But she'd moved it whilst checking if he was breathing and it was *her* gun. The presence of prints wouldn't amount to much in a court of law."

Alice wasn't convinced. "I expect the police think Charmian ditched her clothes and took a shower *after* shooting her husband in the head, getting rid of any residue traces. That would account for the time lag following the reports of a noisy disturbance and the security manager letting himself into the apartment. She had plenty of opportunity."

Kelso stared at the bottom of his empty cup, where just the dark stain of his espresso remained. "Yeah, that's just what I thought you might say."

Chapter 3

The string quartet finished up its set with the violinist performing a surprisingly folksy tune that reminded Dani of the many nights she'd spent with her father in their cosy local pub on Colonsay.

The fiddler dragged out the final note with an exaggerated movement of his bow. His fellow musicians jumped to their feet with a flourish. The room erupted in applause.

James Irving glanced at his companion, giving her a wary grin. "Did you enjoy it?"

"Of course, the playing was wonderful."

"Would you like to meet the musicians?"

"I'd love to." Dani allowed James to lead her into an adjoining room, smaller and less elaborately decorated that the one which hosted the concert but cosier and holding a set of what looked like regency high-backed sofas and chairs.

The quartet were already there, surrounded by guests in black tie and evening gowns. The throng seemed to automatically part for James, who found his way comfortably to the man who'd been playing the violin so beautifully.

"Howell, what a fantastic final piece, we just loved it!" James shook the tall, lean man by the hand. "Let me introduce my partner, Dani."

Howell Sullivan turned his pale blue eyes towards her. "I'm very pleased to meet you. James has spoken about you often, and with a great deal of affection."

Dani smiled and leant forward so that he could

place his surprisingly cold lips against her cheek. "Thank you so much for inviting us to the recital. I rarely get the chance to enjoy such exquisite music." Her words were entirely genuine.

"People don't often make time for classical concerts. They believe it will be expensive to buy tickets or require extensive forward planning. Playing as part of the *Gaelic Quartet*, we mostly get corporate parties in the audience – not that we would complain about that, of course. Every musician is just pleased to be heard."

"That's why I try to come along to a concert whenever Howell is in town. I knew he was a talented bugger, even when we were at school."

Howell raised his eyebrows. "The tutors at the Scott Academy were always trying to encourage me to focus more on my academic studies. But to no avail. They had pupils like James to excel in that area."

James grabbed a couple of flutes of champagne from a passing waiter and handed one to Dani, offering the other to his friend.

Howell shook his head good-naturedly. "No thank you. I'm driving this lot back to Helensburgh tonight."

Dani was surprised. "Don't you have a driver for that kind of thing?" The DCI knew that Howell Sullivan was coming to the end of a three-month long tour of Scotland. Before that he had been gigging around Australia, where his album of solo pieces had reached number one in the classical charts.

Howell laughed. "Only when I'm performing the classical stuff for Turntable Records. That's the work that pays my bills. The gigs I perform with these guys are purely for fun." He gestured towards the smartly dressed man and two ladies who made up the quartet. "Or for charity, like this evening."

James placed his hand on Howell's back. "We'll duck out and head home; give you a chance to mingle with these corporate types. They should be able to donate a decent chunk of cash to the cause."

Howell nodded. "Sure, that's what we're all really here for." He dipped his head towards Dani. "It certainly was a pleasure to meet you at last."

*

James was guiding his BMW carefully through the dark streets of Glasgow. The wipers were clearing off a constant smir of rain to a hypnotic rhythm. "I knew you'd enjoy Howell's music. Whenever I see him perform live, he throws in some of the fiddle music I remember him for when we were students."

"He's incredibly talented. I can see why he's had so much success." Dani straightened her velvet skirt. "Thanks for taking me along."

Since James Irving's involvement in a case Dani had investigated a few months earlier, their relationship had been going through what could only be described as a trial period. The trust that had previously existed between them had been sorely tested. The jury was still out on whether they would ever fully regain it.

He leant a hand across to rest briefly on hers. "Not a problem. I want us to try and do more stuff like this together."

Dani shifted a little awkwardly at his touch. "So, Howell raises money for the Birth Anomaly Trust. How long has he been involved with the charity?"

James slid his hand back onto the wheel. "About seven years. Ever since Dolly was born."

"She was his daughter?"

"Yep, she lived for six months."

"What about the girl's mother?"

"The relationship didn't survive the grief of losing the baby."

"It's a common story, I'm afraid." Dani sighed heavily. "What exactly was wrong with Dolly?"

"Caz gave birth about three weeks prematurely. Dolly had a low birth weight, as you would imagine, but there were also defects to her respiratory and digestive system. She was never able to be taken home. Dolly needed constant care and a feeding tube administered by hospital staff."

"But she lived for six months?"

"Yes, the poor wee thing made decent progress, she'd gradually put on weight and gained good muscle strength. But a bout of pneumonia was too much for her respiratory system. It took her quickly and painlessly." James couldn't help but feel it had been for the best. Although, he knew better than to ever voice this opinion. Dolly had defects in all her major organs that would have meant many long operations and a limited quality of life, possibly leaving her in constant pain. He shook the disturbing memory from his mind. "Howell started campaigning the day after the funeral. He'd just signed up with Turntable Records and was becoming reasonably well-known as an artist. He was able to use his growing fame to raise considerable sums for the cause."

"The charity focusses on research and raising awareness of babies with problems like Dolly's?"

"That's right. There can be any number of different causes, including pre-maturity. But the Trust is researching means of prevention through better ante-natal care and advice, along with expertise and specialist equipment for maternity units after birth. I've done some legal work for them over the years."

Dani knew this would have been free of charge.

James was a good man. "I suppose grief affects folk in different ways. Dad and I never considered working with PND charities after what happened with Mum. Maybe we should have."

James stared out at the grey streets. "I'm not so sure it would have been a good idea. I've often thought that Howell has used his charity work as a way of blotting out the grief. He's never confronted it properly. That was Caz's argument too. She didn't care so much about all the babies who were to come after. She just wanted to focus on Dolly's memory."

"And that's what drove them apart in the end?"

James shrugged. "We never really know what's going on in another person's relationship, do we? Howell started touring a lot overseas. Maybe it would have happened anyway." He pulled up alongside the kerb opposite their flat.

Dani clasped James's hand as they approached the front door, leaning her weight onto his arm. "I really did enjoy this evening. I'd like to do something similar again."

James smiled to himself as Dani unlocked the door, a pleasant rush of warm air greeting them. For the time being, he was perfectly happy to settle for that.

Chapter 4

Alice had chosen to stay in one of those places that's usually somebody's house and they rented out when they themselves were on holiday. It was supposed to give you an authentic experience of the city you were visiting.

The flat she'd plumped for was in the Edinburgh suburb of Marchmont. The DCI had recommended the area to her. It was a pleasant street of traditional, sandstone villas split into apartments over three floors. The one Alice was seated in was cosy but well-appointed. She'd spread the case notes that Fergus Kelso had given her across the tiny kitchen table and furnished herself with a large glass of wine.

The only reason Kelso's firm had been granted access to the investigation files was because the Chief of Police had golfed once at St Andrews and had developed an enduring love of Scotland. When the First Minister had requested that Charmian be allowed to consult with a Scottish lawyer, she was in luck. Usually, the Chinese authorities had little time for foreign intervention in its criminal cases.

Alice had to concede that the investigation in Beijing had been conducted thoroughly. The apartment had been forensically tested to rule out the possibility of a third party being present at the time of the shooting. This scenario could be pretty much discounted. Which left them with two working theories. Either Charmian's story was correct, and her husband shot himself whilst his wife was in the shower, or it was Charmian who pulled the trigger, before washing away the traces.

Alice had to admit the evidence pointed to the latter. There was evidence of Zhu Deming's fresh prints on the gun, but his wife could easily have placed them there immediately after the shooting. And Alice could find no evidence in the police interviews with friends and family to suggest that Deming was suicidal. His business was flourishing and his mood upbeat.

The detective couldn't understand why the man would choose the night after returning from a luxury holiday to end his own life. It didn't make sense. Alice had a great deal of sympathy with Kelso. She didn't agree with the death penalty. It was inhumane. Charmian Zhu faced death by firing squad. It was horrific. But each country had their own laws. If you chose to live there, you had to abide by them or face the consequence. There was no doubt in the DI's mind the woman was guilty.

The phone on the table started to buzz. Alice picked it up. It was Kelso. "Hi, I was just reading through the police reports you gave me."

"Any fresh ideas?" His voice held a hint of desperation.

"Sorry, Mr Kelso. I tend to agree with the Beijing police department. There's not enough evidence to support the theory of suicide. To be honest, it also strikes me as far-fetched."

"But from a legal point of view, the onus is on the prosecution to prove beyond doubt that Charmian is guilty. I don't believe the investigation has achieved that. Certainly not sufficiently enough to put her in front of a firing squad."

Alice could tell he was fighting hard to keep his emotions in check. She thought there might even have been a catch in his voice. This case had really got under his skin. "Look. Why don't you come over to the place I'm staying and we can talk it through?"

There was silence on the line for a moment.

"Okay. Let me know the postcode and I'll jump in a cab."

*

Kelso was wearing a light grey sweater and jeans. He'd obviously managed to pick up a bottle of wine from somewhere. The generic brand made Alice assume it was from an express supermarket in the centre of town.

She led him into the compact kitchen. "If this was my own place, I'd offer you a bite to eat. Sadly, the cupboards are bare."

"Not a problem." He sat at the table and expertly opened the bottle he'd brought, noting the half empty one by the sink. "Sorry, did you want to finish that first?"

Alice dropped down onto the seat opposite her guest. "Not really. It was left as a welcoming gift by the guy who owns this place. I'm guessing his usual tipple is beer."

Kelso chuckled. "I appreciate you seeing me in your own time, like this. Whatever you may think, I'm not trying to emotionally blackmail you."

Alice took a swig of the far superior wine her guest had supplied. "For what it's worth, I think for your own sake you need to develop more detachment. Especially in your line of work. It's a lesson you learn hard and fast in the police force."

Kelso grimaced. "Ouch. I was hoping to have come across as the hardened professional."

"Your compassion is very much to your credit. But sometimes a client isn't worth your sleepless nights. People who kill don't feel the same way we do. They don't have empathy for others. You'll be wasting your life crying tears over them."

Kelso thought this young detective was a tough character for her years. "You mean people like Charmian Zhu?"

Alice shrugged. "I'm afraid so. The evidence suggests to me that she killed her husband. The woman is most likely lying to you and has been from the start."

A shadow passed across Kelso's handsome features. He reached for his glass and sipped slowly. "I suppose I wanted a second opinion. I needed another set of eyes on the evidence to ensure I wasn't bending it to suit what I wanted to be the answer."

Alice was genuinely concerned for him. "I'm not saying I know everything. I can discuss it with DCI Bevan too, I realise you trust her implicitly. But I've got a hunch her assessment will be the same as mine."

Kelso nodded slowly. "Yeah, I think you're right. Dani would have told me the exact same thing." He stood abruptly and pushed his chair back. "I'm sorry, I've been an idiot. I shouldn't have come here."

Alice put out a hand to touch his arm. "Come on, it doesn't mean we can't still talk it out. There may be some kinks in the system that you and your firm could exploit. The fact there's a senior officer over in Beijing prepared to work with you is a very positive starting point. Can you find some grounds for extradition? You said she looked in poor health?" The detective wasn't sure why she felt so compelled to help the guy. But there was something appealingly uncynical about him.

Kelso stood very still. "DI Mann, I really appreciate your input. But I haven't been totally straight with you."

Alice looked puzzled. She let her hand drop back down by her side. "How do you mean?"

He cleared his throat, stalling for time. "The case notes, they represent all of the information I have. That much I've shared completely."

Alice frowned. "Go on."

"The woman, Charmian Zhu. I have a connection to her. Someone else at my firm will be heading up the appeal. But it was me who pushed for us to take it on." He dropped back down heavily into the chair, the wine glasses nearly spilling their contents. "The accused. She's my mother."

Chapter 5

They had graduated to the sofa in the lounge which possessed a bay window facing the street. The distant sound of a police siren and the underlying hum of the city was all that broke the silence.

Alice poured out the remainder of the wine between their two glasses. "How long have you known?"

"I was provided with her name when I requested my adoption details when I was twenty. Charmian Wilson gave birth to me at the age of seventeen. I was put up for adoption within only a few days. The decision must have been made before I was even born."

"She was very young. Her parents probably made the call. Charmian went on to study at Oxford University. She must have been very academically bright. I suppose they didn't want their daughter to be an unmarried, single mum."

Kelso nodded. "Sure, I understood. My own parents – my *adoptive* parents – said that it was quite common back in those days for middle class families to give up an illegitimate child. They believed it would provide everyone involved with better prospects for the future."

"In a sense, it did." Alice felt distinctly uncomfortable. She wasn't renowned amongst her colleagues for her bedside manner. "Charmian travelled across the globe and never had a family herself. She clearly wasn't really the maternal type."

"And I had wonderful parents who loved me to bits. I also got the privilege of a great education." He managed a half-smile. "I never had a problem with it before. I looked up Charmian's career in Hong Kong a decade ago and felt genuinely pleased for her. I possessed no desire to get in touch with the woman. I'd thought little or nothing about her in the intervening ten years."

"Then she got arrested for the murder of her husband." Alice knocked back a mouthful of her drink. "How did you find out about it?"

"We receive a copy of the China Daily at our chambers. My birth mother has a unique name. When I read about what had happened to her, I felt compelled to get involved. I made a few calls to find out whether Charmian had been granted access to a Scottish lawyer. The rest followed from there."

Alice sighed. "Does she know you are her birth son?"

Kelso shook his head. "I didn't tell her when I visited her at the prison. She's no way of knowing. With her current state of mind as it is, I think landing that particular bombshell on her would be unwise."

"I agree. To be honest with you, I think you've done enough for her. You've made sure she gets access to excellent legal representation. You don't have any greater responsibility to the woman than that, surely?"

Kelso glanced up and caught Alice's eye. "I wasn't expecting to feel as if I had, but when I met Charmian I felt something – an instant familiarity. I knew instinctively that she was my flesh and blood."

"It must be very difficult to imagine she could kill a man."

He ran a hand through his thick hair. "That's just the problem. I *can't* imagine it. Whatever the evidence suggests, every fibre of my being tells me the woman is innocent." His expression was full of angst. "I've interviewed death row inmates before, it's never been possible for me to make any clear judgment about their guilt. But this meeting was different. I *knew* she was telling the truth."

Alice frowned deeply. "This is exactly why we keep family members out of these situations. The connection skews people's judgement. Your emotions are interfering with your ability to make a rational assessment. You need to hand the case over to your colleagues and try to forget all about it."

Kelso gave a grunt that almost sounded like a laugh. "I'd love to do that Alice – to drop Charmian Zhu from my life and never think about her existence again, but I can't. You must see that? Now I've set eyes on her in that terrible state, in her awful predicament? She's my *mother* for God's sake. I simply can't let it go."

Chapter 6

When DS Calder saw the boss walking past in the direction of her office he raised his head from the computer screen. "Any news on when Alice gets back from Edinburgh, Ma'am?"

Dani paused by his desk. "She's asked for a couple more days of leave. Why, is there a problem?"

Andy sighed. "Not as such. The Fiscal's office is happy to proceed with a charge of producing and distributing extreme pornographic material against Len Dalgleish. The penalty is three to five year's imprisonment. They think the evidence is sufficient to push for the maximum sentence."

"Good. That's the result we all wanted, isn't it?" Dani rested her weight on the edge of the desk.

"Aye, it's just that going back through all the images and correspondence we found in Dalgleish's property showed up some other faces and names, other than just his."

"You think these people might be associates?" Dani was interested.

Andy nodded. "Going back decades, I'd say. But the stuff I found was inconclusive. The Fiscal wants to focus on the man we've got." He scratched his head. "I just thought Alice and I could have one last trawl through the material together. She might spot something I missed. The DI is good at that."

"She certainly is. But by the sounds of things, the search can wait a few days. Dalgleish is safely in custody and he won't get bail now."

"Aye," Andy responded tentatively, "But if he has got mates in the same line of work, they'll be clearing out their operations and crawling back into the woodwork now that they know their associate has been collared. There may only be a small window of opportunity to find the incriminating evidence."

Dani considered this. She gestured to the messy pile of sheets on his desk. "If you put together a comprehensive folder of stuff, in date order if you can, I'll look through it this evening."

Andy beamed. "Thanks Ma'am. I'll do the same myself, see if there isn't something there I didn't pick up on the first time around."

*

James was leaning against the breakfast bar, flicking through the Herald, a pot of coffee by his elbow. Dani filled her own cup from it and glanced over his shoulder at the article he was reading.

"Did Howell's charity recital make the paper?"

"Yes, a tiny write up in the arts section. I reckon he'll be disappointed." James turned back to the front page and pushed it towards her. "The first few columns are dominated by the story of the schoolboy charged with manslaughter over the death of his classmate."

Dani shifted the page round so she could read the by-line. "The case is being handled by Central Division. The school is nearer to Stirling than here. I've spoken to the DCC about the details though."

James looked intrigued. "But the boy's death was a result of an accident during playtime – how can that possibly be deemed *manslaughter*?"

Dani perched on a stool and sipped her drink. "It's a little more complicated than the press have made out. Harry Gill is sixteen and heavily built. He plays rugby for the school's first team. The boy he tackled to the ground was half his size and only thirteen years old. Joshua Garvey received a massive blow to the head as he hit the hard earth. He suffered a huge cranial haemorrhage and was dead before the ambulance even arrived. This Gill lad had a previous history of assaults on other boys."

"But school isn't like the outside world. There's always a certain amount of rough and tumble. It toughens kids up for the future."

Dani looked at her partner carefully. Not for the first time she was made acutely aware of the differences in their backgrounds. "You can't get away with assaulting a minor, it doesn't matter the institution you choose to exercise your bullying within – whether it's a school or a sports club – the law will catch up with you."

"But won't it put parents off allowing their children to take part in competitive sports at school, if they're worried that a misguided tackle might land their kid in prison? We've got enough of an obesity crisis as it is."

Dani knew this was an issue that was important to James, who genuinely felt his character had been formed on the sports fields of his exclusive boarding school. But then again, she also knew he was wrong. "A sport which causes its players serious residual brain injury isn't character building, James. Children can keep fit in ways that doesn't involve the weaker ones being subjected to life-threatening rough contact from the bigger ones. That kind of life lesson went out of fashion in the stone age."

James finished his coffee and stood up. He looked offended. "I'm going for a run. Do you want to join me?"

"No thanks, I want to finish looking through this material for Andy. I promised I'd give it my full attention."

"Fine," he replied, almost petulantly. "I'll be back before lunch."

Dani barely heard the front door banging shut, she was so engrossed in the pile of papers Andy had placed in a paper folder for her. These pieces of correspondence weren't the deeply unpleasant material that the vice squad had sifted through. They were the apparently innocuous letters, photos and snapshots of a 54 year old unmarried bank clerk who in all other respects had lived a fairly ordinary life.

Judging by the order of the letters, Dalgleish had spent a number of his early years in the army. There was a photograph showing a young Len in a line-up of other boys in uniform. Dani decided they were all no more than eighteen years of age. She turned over the dog-eared polaroid and noted the words written in faded biro on the back:

Boys from the 5th Scots, Girdwood Barracks, Belfast. November 1980.

Dani wondered how young Len was when he developed a taste for hard-core porn. It was more difficult to get hold of back in those days. But he and his fellow soldiers must have had a decent stash of top shelf magazines between them, stuffed inside the worn stitching of mattresses and hidden under floorboards in their barracks. They were adolescent lads and away from home for the first time, it was inevitable.

Further through the pile was the evidence of Dalgleish's civilian life. One set of letters in particular caught her attention. Len had obviously been courting a woman in the mid to late eighties. Her first name was Karla but the envelopes were missing so her surname and address remained a mystery. The letters were tenderly written and not at all explicit. They suggested a tentative relationship that had the potential to end in marriage. Then the correspondence abruptly ended, seemingly at a point where things were about to get serious. Karla had mentioned them taking a holiday together and a lunch date with her parents.

Dani flicked through the rest of the contents but found no further reference to Karla. From 1990 onwards, Dalgleish's personal effects related only to the occasional reunion dinner with his old regiment and photos of Len with men of a similar age in beer gardens on sunny days. The DCI wasn't sure there was any evidence amongst the materials that pointed to other associates being involved in Dalgleish's pornography business. If those men in the pictures were dodgy, there was absolutely no way to prove it simply from what lay in her hands.

Scooping up the dog-eared contents and slipping it back into the file, Dani considered suggesting to Calder that he perform some checks with the 5th Scots Regiment and get hold of Dalgleish's service record. Other than that, the DCI felt their investigation had most likely come to an end.

Chapter 7

Alice wasn't one for lying in her bed, even if she didn't have to be in the office. It was still early and the detective could hear the other residents of the flats in the Marchmont villa moving about, getting ready to set off for work. She found the noise reassuring.

Kelso had left at around eleven the previous night. She'd already cleared their glasses and plates into the slimline dishwasher. The lawyer's words were still swimming round in her head.

Alice had been on holiday to Thailand once, but that was the closest she'd been to China and the far-east. She imagined Charmian Wilson making a life for herself over there; marrying a local and no-doubt learning the language. A whole new alphabet and way of writing. It was a culture so very different to their own.

She found it hard to get into the head of this woman who had given up a baby and her remaining family back in Scotland without a second thought. Alice didn't find the idea of her sympathetic. But she liked Fergus Kelso. He was dedicated and serious-minded, very much like her.

The internet carried a certain amount of information relating to the case, mostly obituaries of Charmian's husband, who'd been a prominent Chinese businessman.

Zhu Deming had been the CEO of Asia Trust Management, a company with offices in Beijing, Hong Kong, Kuala Lumpur, New York and London. Deming's family owned an estate in the hills just outside Beijing, with views of the Great Wall itself. This was in addition to the flat the couple shared in the city. Alice noted how the obituaries hinted at a huge inheritance in the offing for Deming's widow following his death.

The DI shook her head in frustration. If Charmian was intending to kill her husband for his money, it would have made little sense to shoot him in a locked apartment where she was the only suspect. Claiming suicide wouldn't have been sensible either, as Deming's life insurance would be invalidated if it were proved the man took his own life.

The planning and executing of the murder suggested Charmian wasn't very clever, yet Alice knew this couldn't be true. Charmian had a first-class degree from Oxford and was a highly successful businesswoman in her own right. She sighed, the case didn't make a great deal of sense.

But if the crime was one of passion; if Deming was abusive towards his wife or conducted affairs that Charmian knew about, the imprecise nature of the killing fitted better. Relations had come to a head on their holiday, the wife could take no more and as soon as they got home to the flat where Charmian had access to her gun, she shot him.

Alice shrugged her shoulders in defeat. Without being able to interview witnesses, friends and family members or view the crime scene, it was impossible for her to draw any further conclusions. She stood up and grabbed her jacket instead, intent on taking in the sites of Edinburgh before returning to Glasgow the following day.

*

Fortunately for Andy Calder, the headquarters of the 5th Battalion of the Royal Regiment of Scotland was situated just north of Glasgow. The grounds were small, but the entrance marked by an impressive stone gateway.

Andy was met by Captain Sutherland, who was expecting his visit. The detective put out his hand as the imposing man in uniform approached the reception desk.

"I'm DS Calder, my DCI spoke with you earlier today. I appreciate you seeing me at such short notice."

Sutherland dipped his head of grey-speckled hair. "Not at all, Detective Sergeant. We are always ready to help the police."

The Captain's office was covered with dark oak panels and the lead-lined windows looked out onto what Andy assumed was a parade ground.

"I'm not sure how much information you will be able to give us. The man we are interested in who served with your regiment must have left the army in the late 1980s."

Sutherland nodded. "I've looked up his service record. Leonard Dalgleish was an infantry soldier with us from late '79 to the August of 1988."

"Nearly a decade," Andy muttered.

"Dalgleish served in Belfast for the majority of that time, as was commensurate with the era. He was just a lad when he joined up and never appears to have sought to rise through the ranks. But our records show he maintained a strong connection to the regiment after he left us. Dalgleish is still on our mailing list for dinners and events."

Andy furrowed his brow. "Did my DCI explain what Dalgleish has been charged with?"

Sutherland sighed heavily. "Yes, she did. It's extremely disappointing. Although, the man had had no proper connection to the regiment for nearly thirty years. I don't see what his present crimes have really got to do with us."

"They don't have anything to do with the regiment, I'm sure. All I want to do is to take a look at Dalgleish's record for myself. As you say, he kept in contact with the regiment and I'm hoping to be able to speak with some of his old army pals. There were pictures of them in his possession, but no names I'm afraid."

Sutherland's mouth fixed in a grim line. "I can let you have access to the records, by all means. His postings over the years will lead you to lists of his fellow soldiers and commanding officers. But I must make it clear that this line of inquiry disturbs me somewhat." He leant forward, broad hands spread across the solid wood desk. "The implication seems to be that Dalgleish possessed criminal associates from within my regiment. I don't much like the insinuation, particularly as no facts back it up."

Calder found himself unable to reply.

"Peruse the lists, by all means. But I'd prefer it if your interest in our institution didn't find its way into the domain of the press."

Calder shook his head. "It won't Sir, I give you my word."

Sutherland narrowed his eyes until they were tiny slits of blackness. The man was apparently assessing just how much Calder's word was actually worth.

Chapter 8

The whitewashed cottage sat in the middle of a terrace of identical houses a couple of streets away from the waterfront.

Howell Sullivan carried a pot of tea into the small conservatory that jutted into the long, thin garden. There was just enough sunlight to have warmed the room. He knew his neighbours in Helensburgh were amazed by the modesty of his lifestyle. Howell was pretty much a household name in his native Scotland.

The cottage had three bedrooms, which allowed for a separate office and music studio. This was all he needed. Howell had no family any longer and had never been much of a cook. He enjoyed the conservatory in summer and the cosy front room in winter. The set-up suited him perfectly. Then, he was free to use the majority of his royalties to keep the charity afloat. With swathing government cuts to health care services south of the border, they were needed now more than ever.

Howell glanced at the mobile phone resting on the glass topped coffee table. He diverted his gaze and poured a cup of tea from the pot, slowly and deliberately. In recent months, the musician had been troubled. Touring abroad helped to take his mind off things, but now he was back home, the worries had resurfaced, this time worse than ever.

Even when it was so cold in the cottage that condensation formed on the inside of the wooden framed windows in his bedroom, Howell would awaken with sweat drenching his sheets and a painful grip in his stomach like a nasty bout of food poisoning. He knew there was no physical cause. Even his music was suffering. He had always been able to blot out every thought and feeling whilst he played. No longer was this the case. Howell's mind would begin to wander during performances, unwanted and unbidden images forced themselves to the forefront of his mind.

Feeling his heartbeat start to quicken, Howell took a gulp of tea to moisten his dry mouth. Then he picked up the mobile phone and quickly dialled, before his sweaty hand had time to falter over the keys.

*

Dani had never seen Andy so engrossed in his paperwork. It was a sign they must both be getting old. Usually, if her DS was utterly absorbed in a case he would be tearing around Glasgow demanding information from people. The last few weeks, he'd decided to put in the groundwork first. She hoped it would earn him results.

The DCI glanced past Calder's desk to the lift, which was opening with a clunky whine. To Dani's great surprise, it was James who stepped out onto the floor of the serious crime division.

She emerged from her office and walked over to meet him. Her boyfriend's expression was grave.

"Is everything okay? Has something happened with your mother?"

James shook his head. "No, nothing like that. But I need to talk to you urgently." He scanned the room nervously. "And it had better be in private."

Dani closed the door behind them. James was

already lowering himself onto the tiny sofa by the filing cabinet.

"I received a phone call."

"From whom?" A feeling of dread was tightening her chest.

"It was Howell Sullivan. He wanted to report a crime. He sounded in an absolute state. He said that he should have called you directly, but he didn't have your number and, truthfully, he wanted to tell me first. *Confess*, I suppose." James ran a hand through his dark hair.

"Confess to what?" Dani narrowed her eyes, wondering where Howell was right now.

James looked up and caught her eye. "Something about his past, from when he was first married. Caz and Howell hadn't been together very long when she fell pregnant. They weren't married and it hadn't been a part of their long-term plan to settle down and have kids. Caz is a professional singer. Back then, she was determined to hit the big-time with her career. You have to be young to be successful in that business."

Dani nodded. "Go on."

"Caz found out she was pregnant in the Autumn of 2009. She didn't tell another soul at first. It wasn't what she wanted at that time in her life, the discovery was most unwelcome. The girl panicked, I suppose. She was worried Howell would be angry with her for being so careless, that he might even leave her." James went pale. "Rather than confront reality, one night Caz took a cocktail of drugs and alcohol, hoping it would make the problem disappear – one way or the other."

"Was she trying to kill herself?"

"Howell isn't sure, but Caz threw up some hours later and that's probably what saved her."

Dani's mind was ticking over fast. "But what

about the baby?"

"Caz woke up the next day feeling like total shit, but glad to be alive and with a better perspective on things. She went for a scan a week later and everything seemed okay."

"They can't tell much from those early ultrasounds," Dani said gravely.

"Then Caz told Howell about the pregnancy and he was actually overjoyed. Everything went as normal after that, until a month before the due date. Then Caz started having serious cramps and the midwife said the baby wasn't thriving. She was induced at thirty-seven weeks."

"And the baby girl was born with all those awful complications," Dani said quietly.

"Howell knew nothing about the drink and drug binge until after Dolly died. Then Caz told him the whole sorry tale."

"No wonder they didn't stay together." Dani poured them both a cup of water from the dispenser.

James sipped it gratefully. "The charity thing has been a way for Howell to deal with the guilt."

"It wasn't really his fault." Dani placed her hand on James's knee. "Does Howell believe that Caz committed a crime?"

James creased his face. "I'm not entirely sure. I suppose he's tortured with not knowing whether it was the botched attempt to get rid of the baby that caused her all those disabilities, or Dolly was always going to be that way. *He* believes Caz is responsible for his daughter's death, that much is certain."

Dani sat back against the thin cushions. "I suspect that medically it would be impossible to prove. I'm positive no laws have been broken. Abortion is legal up to 28 weeks of pregnancy. I expect plenty of women drink heavily in the early part of the first trimester. Many won't even know they're expecting."

James shook his head. "I suppose you're right. But morally, it's a bloody minefield. Caz must be aware she probably caused all those developmental defects in the child."

Dani sighed sadly. "Sometimes people have ways of protecting themselves from the truth. I expect Caz has persuaded herself now that there was no link between the two events, especially if the medics didn't make the connection at the time."

"Howell says that a big part of their charity work is aimed at educating couples about the dangers of alcohol and drug abuse during pregnancy. He's made himself an expert on the symptoms and manifestations of F.A.S."

"Foetal Alcohol Syndrome. We come across it occasionally with some of the repeat offenders whose mothers were alcoholics. The signs aren't always obvious until the child reaches later life, although sufferers are often disruptive at school and fail to gain any qualifications."

"Christ. The cards are stacked against these poor buggers before they're even born."

Dani straightened in her seat. "Rhodri Morgan has worked with several clients who have been diagnosed with F.A.S. He's got a great deal of clinical expertise in that area. Perhaps Howell should talk to the professor about his experience. I think Rhodri could help."

James nodded. "Yeah, I'll suggest that. Howell was acting like he'd been living with the knowledge of a murder for all these years."

"For him, that's probably exactly how it felt. He's suffered in his own form of prison for the last seven years – even real murderers don't necessarily serve for that long."

James rose to his feet, a determined expression

on his face. "You're right, it's not fair. I'm going to do something about it."

"Good. But before you do," Dani added in a steely tone, "I'd be interested to know Caz's full name."

Chapter 9

The sky was the clearest blue over Edinburgh Castle, but the air was crisp and cold. Alice zipped her thick fleece up to the neck, conscious that her nose would be bright red.

Her companion hadn't said much during their walk around the older part of the city. His hands were pushed down into the pockets of his padded body-warmer and his vision fixed dead ahead. The detective wasn't quite sure what had prompted her to call the lawyer up and ask him to accompany her.

Alice glanced in his direction. "Do you want to head up to the castle?"

Fergus shrugged. "Aye, we could take a walk around the walls, but I don't much fancy the full guided tour."

"No, neither do I. The fresh air is helping me to think."

Fergus shot her a look in return. "Any sparkling revelations DI Mann?"

"I'm considering my future position, that's all. Now I've gained my inspector rank, I can take up the role wherever there's a vacancy."

"Have you got roots in Glasgow?" He paused, "anyone keeping you in the city?"

"No, not at all. My parents live out in Largs and they aren't getting any younger. But I can easily visit them from somewhere else in Scotland."

The pair stopped walking and absorbed the view as the gradient took them gradually above the skyline.

"Then now may be a good time to spread your wings. I've travelled a great deal for my cases. At first

I loved it, but the novelty wears off." Fergus gazed into the distance wistfully. "There comes a time when you naturally want to settle. Roots become more important to you."

"I love my parents dearly, but I've always felt most comfortable on the job. My team are like family to me. It's them I don't want to leave."

"DCI Bevan you mean?"

She nodded. "And Dan Clifton – even Calder. We've been through a lot of stuff that other people wouldn't understand."

Fergus shifted closer and took her hand. "Maybe I would?"

Alice examined his face, the deep brown eyes and earnest brow. "Yes, maybe you would."

*

Professor Rhodri Morgan was shuffling papers around the large oak desk in the spare room of his Kelvingrove flat. Despite preparing to retire from his teaching role at the university that summer, Rhodri felt like he was as busy as he'd ever been. The sound of the entrance buzzer actually came as a welcome intrusion.

When the professor saw it was Dani on his doorstep, he was even more receptive to the interruption. He even ventured out to meet her on the wide, communal staircase.

"Danielle, what a pleasure to see you!"

Dani couldn't help but smile and fold herself into the older man's embrace. "I'm really sorry to bother you in the daytime. The university switchboard told me you were working from home today."

Rhodri nodded vigorously as he ushered her inside. "The principal has reduced my teaching load for my final couple of terms. I do my paperwork from here two days a week."

"You're definitely leaving academia then?" Dani shook off her jacket and took a seat at the kitchen table.

"I will miss the students terribly, but not the bureaucracy." He rummaged around in a cupboard for coffee cups. "I will be continuing my clinical work, and I remain on the list of experts available to the police."

"I'm glad to hear it."

"In fact, I'm rather busy at the moment."

Dani's face fell. "Oh, I was hoping to ask for your help with something."

"Is it one of your cases?"

"No, it isn't." Dani took a deep breath and relayed Howell Sullivan's history to the professor.

Rhodri busied himself preparing the coffee, whilst clearly listening carefully to what he was being told.

Dani sipped the bitter liquid. "Well, do you think you could help him?"

Rhodri lowered himself onto the seat opposite. "This is a peculiar coincidence."

Dani furrowed her brow. "How come? Do you know Howell?"

He shook his head of loose grey hair. "No, and I'm not familiar with his music either." The professor twisted his cup. "It's the issues involved." He shifted forward. "Are you familiar with the Harry Gill case?"

"The boy being charged with manslaughter over the death of his classmate?" She nodded. "Central are handling it, but I've been briefed by the DCC."

"I've been asked to review the case by the family's defence team."

"In what capacity?" Dani was intrigued. She knew this was what Rhodri did for a living and wasn't at all put out.

"I'm telling you this in your capacity as a senior

police officer. It can go no further."

"Of course."

"Harry – or Hal, as he is known to friends and family, has a rather chequered past. He has been disciplined by his fee-paying secondary school on a number of occasions for violent behaviour towards fellow pupils and staff. He also suffers from dyslexia and slow processing skills." Rhodri placed his palms flat on the table between them. "His parents contacted me directly, because of my clinical expertise. Apparently, the boy's birth mother died when he was four year's old. Sarah Gill is his step-mother. Colin informed me that his first wife was an alcoholic and this was what killed her."

Dani blinked vigorously, the pieces beginning to fall together. "His parents think Hal was born with Foetal Alcohol Syndrome."

Rhodri nodded solemnly. "They want all the necessary tests carried out. A positive result would provide the boy with mitigation in court."

"How easy is it to diagnose the condition?"

"There are tests that can be carried out to highlight cognitive deficits and executive functioning limitations – that's stuff like displaying poor judgement, or an inability to appreciate cause and effect."

"Like every criminal I've ever come across," Dani put in.

"Quite so. It makes one wonder about the background of most violent offenders." He ran a hand through his hair, leaving it even messier than before. "The hospital can also run a CT scan. They look for anomalies in brain structure that indicate FAS."

"Do you have a result for the boy yet?"

Rhodri sighed. "The brain scan was inconclusive. In severe cases, the skull will be smaller than normal, in lesser cases there will be subtle changes in the structure of the brain which point to FAS. With Hal, there were some structural abnormalities but they were within the margin of error. The prosecuting council could also argue the damage to the brain is the result of his long-term rugby playing, rather than anything that occurred in the womb."

"I see. So, will it be possible to form a decent defence on the basis of FAS?"

Rhodri grimaced. "I will put together a report based on my assessments and interviews. I've no doubt the lad has an impaired mental capacity, but whether it is sufficient to excuse causing the death of a child, I'm really not sure."

Dani nodded. She knew the professor well, he tended to sympathise with the offender in these situations. His comments on the Gill case suggested to her that Hal was most likely a very nasty piece of work. "Do you think you would have the time to speak with Howell? Perhaps your expertise and advice would provide him with some comfort?"

Rhodri shook the Gill case from his mind, as if he were repelling a particularly persistent wasp buzzing around his head. "Of course. Ask him to email me over the next few days to organise a session. I believe I can certainly help the poor man."

Chapter 10

Alice shifted onto her side in bed and allowed her eyes to pass over the hump in the covers made by Fergus Kelso's long, lean frame. She hadn't expected anyone else to be sharing her rental flat during this stay. The room was whitewashed and lacking in any kind of personalisation. She supposed this meant that Fergus still didn't know a great deal about the real Alice.

Sensing her gaze upon him, Fergus opened his eyes and smiled. "Did you forget I was here?"

Alice chuckled. "*No,* I was just thinking how long it was since I'd had a man in my bed. This isn't a familiar scenario for me."

He levered himself up onto an elbow. "Me, either," he added indignantly. "A *woman,* I mean."

She leant forward and placed a kiss on his lips. "I know what you mean."

He pulled back, a frown creasing out from his eyes, which had clouded again with sadness. "You'll be heading back to Glasgow now, I expect. There's no more you can do to assist me."

Alice slid a hand under the covers, searching out the warm gap between his thighs. "I don't know about that..." she murmured. Fergus shuddered and then the entire bedside table started to vibrate.

"Shit, that's mine." Fergus leant across and hooked up his phone. "Kelso," he barked into it.

Alice took the opportunity to use the en-suite bathroom. When she re-entered, Fergus had placed the phone back on the table.

"Is everything okay?" She sensed a distinct change of atmosphere in the room.

He shrugged his shoulders. "That was one of the clerks at my chambers. They've had a call from the Beijing police department. The mayor has set a date for Charmian's execution." Fergus had turned deathly pale.

"When is it?" Alice had a growing sense of foreboding.

"The last Saturday of this month."

*

Fergus had gone straight into the shower and quickly dressed. Alice was still in her nightgown when the lawyer entered the tiny kitchen and gratefully received the cup of coffee she handed him.

He leant against the counter-top and sipped thoughtfully. "It's unusual for local officials to even give us notice ahead of an execution. Often, we find out after the event, when there's nothing more anyone can do about it."

Alice found herself wondering if that might have been better in this case, too. But she said nothing.

Fergus ran a hand through his thick hair. "I didn't think it would hit me like this."

"She is your mother," Alice commented quietly.

He put down his cup on the counter with a thud. "I've got to do something more," he announced. "I'm going to fly back out there."

Alice nodded, already sensing this was coming. "I wish you all the best with your efforts to save her," she said resignedly, lamenting how most of her burgeoning love affairs seemed to end in a similarly abrupt yet blameless way.

Kelso stepped forward and clasped her hands. "I know this is a ridiculous thing to ask, but would you consider coming with me? Perhaps you could extend your leave by a week or so? I could really do with your help on the appeal." He looked sheepish, "and I'm kind of enjoying your company."

"To *China*?" Alice took a step back. Thoughts were bombarding her brain. She had to take a deep breath and remind herself that she had no ties here in Scotland. Nobody could prevent her taking a holiday, not even DCI Bevan. She caught his eye and slowly nodded. "Okay, I'll see what I can do. But I'll need a visa won't I? Can it be organised at this short notice?"

Kelso looked hugely relieved. "If you give me your passport I can sort that out for us. You'll just need to go back to your flat in Glasgow and pick up some more stuff. Then we'll be ready to go."

Chapter 11

Len Dalgleish had spent almost a decade serving out of the Girdwood Barracks in Belfast. He was still only a teenager when he was posted there in early 1979.

Calder had generated a list of fellow infantry soldiers from the service records that Captain Sutherland had provided him with. The DS had started with the men who served for the longest stretches of time alongside Dalgleish. He ended up with a shortlist of four.

None of these men were still serving in the army. A couple had become security specialists – one out in Dubai and the other in London. Calder checked their websites and social media accounts. They appeared to be busy, family men. Not the kind of low paid loner he would expect to be assisting Dalgleish in his sordid pornography business.

The other two were more likely contenders. Ken Garfield was 58 years old and lived in a suburb of south Glasgow, within 10 miles of Dalgleish. Robert Addison was nearing sixty and had a house on the Isle of Mull.

For reasons of convenience, Calder was standing on Garfield's doorstep, examining the exterior of the semi-detached property. He finally pressed the bell.

A woman in her thirties opened up. She was in jogging bottoms and a t-shirt, with a mug of tea in her hand and the collar of a small, scruffy dog in the other.

Calder held out his card. "I'm DS Calder from the Glasgow police. Is your father at home?"

The woman creased her brow. "My Da lives on

the Crosshouse Estate. You've made a mistake, love."

Andy realised he had made a mistake, but it wasn't that. "I'm looking for Ken Garfield. This is his address?"

Realisation seemed to dawn on the woman. "Aye, this is Ken's place. We live here together. I pay the mortgage now, mind. So, I've every right to be here."

Andy put up a placatory hand. "I'm not bothered about that. I just want to find Ken, is he in?" The DS peered over her shoulder into the dingy corridor. He couldn't make out much beyond an overfilled coat rack.

"Ken went on a job in his truck three weeks ago. He hasn't come back."

"Where was he heading?"

She shrugged her narrow shoulders. "Somewhere in Germany. I think it was Kiel. He was getting on a ferry anyways. He called from Harwich but I've not had no message since."

"When was he due back?" Calder was puzzled by her lack of concern.

"A job like that usually takes ten days." She let go of the dog who'd got bored sniffing Calder's shoes and padded back into the house. "But he can be longer than that, especially if he's gone abroad."

Calder nodded. They clearly had the kind of relationship where Garfield disappeared for months at a time. "Is three weeks an unusual amount of time for him to be away?"

Her face suddenly looked pained. "Aye, it is. Especially with no phone call. I assumed he'd left me."

"Have you reported Ken missing? Contacted his family members?"

She shook her head defiantly. "The bastard's done this once too often to warrant that. Besides, he's got no family but me and Rusty. His folks died years back and his sister's down south somewhere."

"I'm going to need to take the details of Ken's place of employment and have a look through his belongings, then I'll have to file a report with missing persons."

"Fine. Go ahead. I was going to contact ma' solicitor anyways, see if I could get the house signed over to me."

Calder said nothing, he'd been involved in these types of cases before. He didn't much rate her chances.

*

"After Natalie Flynn finally allowed me on the premises, I went through Garfield's office in the spare room." Calder flicked through his notebook.

"Any signs of a connection to Dalgleish? That *is* our main priority," Dani said firmly.

"Not amongst his work papers, Ma'am. Garfield was a truck driver for Murray's Haulage up until the end of last year. It seems like he quit the job back then, omitting to mention this fact to his common law."

"Garfield wasn't on a delivery to Kiel at all? He's simply taken off?" Dani rested her weight on the desk.

"Aye, Ma'am. Around the same time we busted Dalgleish."

"There's no proof of a link, Andy. I'm assuming the house showed no sign of having been used to produce or distribute pornography?"

Andy slowly shook his head. "No, but then I believe Garfield would have kept his girlfriend out of it, she hadn't a clue about what he was up to."

"But it's Garfield's property? All the deeds and

bills are in his name?"

"That's right."

"Then why do a disappearing act, leaving the place to Flynn? Especially if there's no criminal evidence in the property. Garfield would have been better off staying there if he was expecting a call from us. We wouldn't have found anything."

Calder appeared sheepish. "I don't know, Ma'am. That's why I've got to keep digging." He gave his boss an imploring look. "When can I get Alice back to give me a hand? I've got a missing person now, and I need to check out the other men on my list."

Dani got to her feet. "Alice has requested another week's leave. She's certainly owed it. I could hardly refuse, particularly as she's well within her rights to take up her inspector position at another station. I want to give her time to make the right decision."

"Alice loves it here, she isn't going to leave us." He rubbed his chin in frustration. "Where's she going, anyway? It's an odd time to take a holiday."

"She's going to China, to assist an appeal team on the case of a Scottish citizen sentenced to death for the murder of a Beijing businessman."

Calder straightened up. "That's a joke, right?"

Dani shook her head, suddenly wishing it was. "Nope, I asked her to answer some questions for Fergus Kelso, as a favour to me."

Despite his bad mood, Calder started to laugh. "Well, it seems like she's ended up doing a bloody sight more than that!"

"Yes," Dani replied through gritted teeth. "It certainly does."

Chapter 12

The he apartment was exactly as Alice had pictured it to be. The kitchen and living areas were open plan and faced a bank of floor to ceiling windows giving an impressive view of downtown Beijing.

The bedrooms and en-suite were situated beyond a connecting door and hallway. Since the death of Zhu Deming, the flat had been sealed off and unused. Although, Kelso had informed her, it was no longer under the restrictions of the police department and the Zhu family had brought in professional cleaners.

Alice approached the windows, which, at closer proximity, she saw were sliding doors leading to a narrow balcony. She tried one of them, to discover it was locked. "The flat feels higher up than I imagined."

Fergus moved over to stand beside her. "Yes, it's hard to imagine anyone getting in or out via the balcony."

"And the sliding doors were locked," Alice added.

"That's right."

Alice turned and scanned the room, imagining the spot where Deming was found, in a pool of blood, the gun on a rug a few feet from his right hand. She looked at the smooth, parquet floor. "What happened to the rug?"

Fergus thought for a moment. "I believe the police took it away as evidence. The cleaners will have polished this floor since."

Alice raised an eyebrow. "They'll still be plenty of

blood down there." She pressed her court shoe against the parquet. "It will have seeped between the strips of wood and into the very grain itself. Perpetrators often think they can get rid of all traces with some bleach and a mop. They're quite wrong."

Fergus shuddered. "I'm surprised they didn't rip the whole floor up. The family can certainly afford it."

"They're probably preparing to sell it, as soon as all the publicity dies down. Then it will be somebody else's problem." Alice stepped towards the spot where the body had lain. "I'm no interior designer, but somehow I don't quite picture a rug in this place. The family obviously haven't replaced it."

"Bad connotations, I suppose. I hadn't thought about it really. Does it matter?"

"Probably not." Alice examined the intercom system, which was positioned on the wall next to the front door. There was a button for the security manager and the reception desk in the foyer.

Fergus glanced at his watch. "We'd better go. The family only granted us an hour. We were lucky to get that."

"Sure," Alice hauled her bag up onto her shoulder. "We should go and check into our hotel anyway."

*

Fergus had been given a small budget for the trip, but it needed to stretch to the two of them. The hotel they chose was the type that students and backpackers might frequent. But Alice found it clean and functional. The police files and scene photographs were laid out on the plain sheets of the bed.

Alice retrieved the photos of the evidence taken

from the Zhu apartment. She peered closely at the shag-pile rug the gun had been found lying on. "I can't see any blood stains on the rug," she muttered, almost to herself.

"The lab reports found a few spatters on it, but the rug was made from one of those synthetic fibres that has been treated to repel stains. Added to the textured surface, the techs couldn't lift much from it."

Alice frowned, she was thinking about the expensively furnished apartment, with natural wood floors that were designed for their aesthetics rather than their practicality. "I just can't imagine Charmian and Deming buying a synthetic rug for that flat."

Fergus glanced up from the report he was reading. "Well, it was there, pure and simple. You can't argue with the facts."

Alice nodded. "Of course, but its existence is an anomaly. That's the kind of detail we look for as detectives. We may not understand yet what it indicates, but it's something to bear in mind."

Fergus still looked sceptical. He picked up the report he was reading instead. "This is the statement given by Deming's older sister. She lives out on the coast with her husband and grown-up children, a few hundred kilometres away from here. The police took longer to interview her than the rest of the family. These files were only given to me yesterday. She claims that her brother was acting differently in the months leading up to his death. Deming seemed pre-occupied and stressed during their phone calls. He talked about maybe leaving the city and starting afresh."

"With or without Charmian?"

"The woman doesn't say."

Alice sighed. "We need to be careful with that

evidence. The sister is commenting several weeks after the event, when she has had time to formulate ideas and theories about what happened to her brother. She may not necessarily be *lying*, but the brain can do strange things after a traumatic incident, like the death of a loved one. People like to find explanations, it helps them to cope."

Fergus leant back on his hands. "I'm not sure the testimony really helps Charmian's case anyway."

Alice gently brushed her lips against his. "When is your visit with her?"

"Tomorrow afternoon."

The detective straightened up, a look of determination on her face. "Then we need to make it as worthwhile as we can. We'll require a brand new set of questions. Let's get to work."

Chapter 13

The two detective constables worked at the station in Tobermory. This visit took one of them back to the south-west side of the island, where his parents had their farm. He pointed out as much to his colleague during the long, twisting drive.

Finally, they pulled up outside the driveway that led to the farmhouse. Mull was a large island, but only a limited part of it was inhabited, the rest an undulating shrubland of forest and hills.

Robert Addison's small-holding was set back from the main road on a dirt track. The main building was modest, but a kitchen extension on the side and a selection of outbuildings made the property seem more substantial.

DC Lowther pressed the bell. There was nothing but silence beyond the paint-peeled front door.

DC Black strode around the building, peering through grubby windows and trying any handle he could find. The place looked untidy but lived in. There were dishes in the sink and mugs hanging on hooks by the kettle. "Looks like someone's living here," he called back to Lowther. "Maybe Addison is up in the hills at the back somewhere."

"Aye," his colleague replied sulkily. "But let's check out these sheds first, before we start scouring the hills and glens."

"Did the Glasgow division provide a description of the man?" Black enquired, striding round to join his fellow officer.

"No, just a name and address. I looked him up

before we set out, mind. Addison runs a repair business out of these barns – fixes lawnmowers, farm machinery and the like."

"Can't make much of a living."

"That's true enough."

They approached the largest of the out-buildings. Two huge corrugated iron sheets were secured with a padlock.

"Must be where he keeps his tools," Black commented.

Lowther shook the metalwork vigorously and a gap formed where one of the sheets met the wooden side of the barn. It was just large enough for the men to squeeze through.

It was dark inside. If there were any windows, Lowther assumed they'd been boarded up.

Black felt the wall behind them for a switch. His hand discovered a surprisingly smooth, modern switch casing. He turned on the light.

Lowther unconsciously took a step backwards as he absorbed the unexpected scene. Lighting equipment, of the sort you'd find on film-sets were placed in front of a line of ordinary double-beds, their sheets silky in appearance and coloured in luxuriant reds and golds.

DC Black let out a gasp. "No wonder Glasgow were so interested in this guy. He's been running a porno studio from up here."

Lowther's age and experience were making him less awe-struck by the discovery. His over-riding sensation was one of dread. "We'll have to get more officers down here to secure the scene."

"Aye, I'll radio them right now." Black squeezed himself back through the gap to make the call.

Lowther stepped cautiously past the equipment, trying to ignore the piles of lingerie and cosmetics that filled a table against the far wall. That kind of evidence was for the likes of the vice squad, not him. Moving closer to the beds, Lowther's eyes were scanning for the strange thing he'd noticed from the entrance. All the sheets were messy, but one of the beds seemed to be sporting a human-shaped mound beneath one of the swathes of gold silk.

When he reached the right place, Lowther took a deep breath and pulled back the material. The contrast struck him immediately. The body of a slightly over-weight, middle-aged man in grubby clothes lying contorted beneath the fine silk, the left side of his skull caved in, dried blood adding an additional pattern to the red sheet covering the mattress.

Lowther sighed, glad that young Black hadn't been the one to make the grisly discovery. Despite the DC's swagger, he was still just a boy, and this wasn't the sort of thing that the island police were very often confronted with.

*

As she surveyed the meeting room, DCI Bevan was made starkly aware of how understaffed she currently was. Without Phil or Alice, she hardly had the kind of investigative team that could handle a murder case.

Calder addressed the team. "As part of my inquiries into the associates of Leonard Dalgleish, I requested that a couple of officers on Mull pay a visit to the property of Robert Addison, a man who served in the army with Dalgleish for the best part of a decade." He turned to indicate the crime scene photos displayed on the screen behind him. "The local boys found a right little sordid treasure trove."

"A studio for producing pornography, Sir?" DC Dan Clifton chipped in.

"Aye, and a sophisticated one at that. There were webcams set-up all over the barn and digital cameras too. We've got a tech team over there going through the place right now, alongside our colleagues from Vice." Andy paused. "But the real discovery for us was the body of Kenneth Garfield of Clyde Road, Glasgow. His head had been caved in by a heavy object. The local doc thought it was most likely one of the metal light stands. We're having them all tested."

Dani addressed the team, "Garfield was another associate of Dalgleish's, missing for the last three weeks. Garfield's dead body was found in one of Addison's sheds, bludgeoned with one of his film lights. Now the man himself is unaccounted for. We have to assume he's our number one suspect for the murder."

"The guys on Mull were more than happy to hand the case back to us. They don't have the experience for something like this, let alone the manpower."

Dani wondered if they really did either. "The ferry terminal employees are checking all passengers leaving for Oban. We've got officers from Highlands and Islands at the other end."

"Are we expecting Addison to still be on the island, Ma'am?" Dan asked incredulously. "How long had Garfield's body been there?"

Andy answered this, "until the *PM* we won't know for sure, but the doc said a week at the most, probably a few days. So, you're right, Dan. Chances are our man is long gone."

"Then we need to check the passenger lists of the ferry going back three weeks. Let's see if we can pin-point when Garfield arrived and when Addison left," Bevan said.

"Sure," Andy replied swiftly. "I'll get onto Cal Mac."

Dani sighed. "The Fiscal will have to delay Dalgleish's prosecution until we sort this mess out. There's no doubt the man was part of something far bigger."

Andy nodded but said nothing. He'd known this much all along.

Chapter 14

Alice hadn't had much cause to imagine what a Chinese prison would look like. They were on a kind of industrial complex a few kilometres outside of Beijing. The prison buildings were surrounded by high walls and barbed wire fences. But it was smaller than the Scottish detective had expected.

Fergus had been through the process before. Alice left him to speak with the reception desk officers and produce all the papers. She was being treated like one of the legal team and thought it best to play along.

Finally, they were transferred to a small room with a desk and chairs in the centre. The walls were tiled right up to the ceiling and a plug hole was fitted into a dip in the concrete floor in one corner. Alice wondered what it was there to wash away. For the first time since arriving in that place, she felt her heart pound in her chest and sweat spring to her brow.

She jumped as the door abruptly opened. Fergus shot her a concerned glance. Then their attention was drawn to the people who entered.

Charmian Zhu was in handcuffs, although her wrists were so bony it looked as if they might slip off at any moment. Her posture was stooped and the two female guards accompanying her seemed almost to be propping her up.

The prisoner dropped into the chair in front of them. Fergus leant forward, his hands involuntarily reaching out to the fragile, shell of a woman seated opposite. "Mrs Zhu, I'm Fergus Kelso from Castle Street Chambers in Edinburgh. I came to visit you a few months back. Do you remember?"

Charmian lifted her eyes. A flicker of recognition showed in their blue depths. She nodded.

"Are you being treated properly? You don't look very well."

"The food doesn't agree with me," she muttered through dry lips. "They treat me well enough."

Alice glanced at each of the guards. Their expressions were fixed and impassive.

"Are you aware that a date has been set for your execution?" Fergus had no way to soften the words, so he let them hang in the air like an unpleasant odour.

"Yes. The governor told me himself." She straightened up a little, tipping her head back to reveal a weary but determined face. "I am ready for what is to come."

"We want to ask you some more questions, Mrs Zhu. There is still time to submit our appeal," Fergus pressed.

"I don't see the point."

Alice leant forward. "What do you mean by that, Mrs Zhu?"

Charmian narrowed her eyes. "I'm not changing my plea, if that's what you're asking. But the evidence is against me. It would be a waste of time to try and fight it."

"We aren't prepared to give up just yet," Fergus added.

"I don't see why," Charmian said levelly. "Everyone else has." Then she looked at him at little oddly, as if seeing the man properly for the first time. "Do I know you – from before all this, I mean? Have we met before?"

Fergus cleared his throat. "Not to my knowledge,

no."

Alice decided to intervene, feeling time slipping away from them. "How well do you know your sister-in-law, Mrs Zhu?"

"Lui? I've not seen her for maybe eighteen months. She lives outside of Beijing with her family. But she and Deming were close. They messaged each other a lot."

"Because Lui claims that your husband was unusually stressed in the weeks leading up to his death. Did Deming have work worries during that time? Were there strains in your marriage?"

Charmian winced, as if the suggestion caused her pain.

"I'm sorry to be so blunt, Mrs Zhu. But we don't have much time. If we are going to find out what really happened to your husband, you're going to have to answer some difficult questions."

The woman nodded, as if the harsh words had brought her out of a trance. "Despite what the police have been insinuating, Deming and I were very happy in our marriage. We were both people who enjoyed our jobs and the luxuries it brought us. There were no affairs or disagreements."

Fergus cut in, "then what about your husband's work? He was the CEO of a major company. There must have been stresses associated with that."

Charmian sighed heavily. "Of course, but Deming always thrived on the pressure. Although, now I'm forced to face the fact he was hiding his stress from me, otherwise why would he have shot himself? He must have opened up to Lui but not to me, his own wife. I don't understand why, but I must simply accept it."

"What were Deming's recent work projects?" Alice persisted.

Charmian crinkled her brow in thought. "Deming

had brought in a big new client, that's why we had decided to take the holiday when we did. It was a businessman based in Kuala Lumpur. He decided to place his investments with Asia Trust Management. It was quite a coup."

"Can you recall his name?"

Charmian concentrated hard but shook her head. "I'm sorry, Deming didn't really go into the specifics with me. I know he was an American, but that's all. You need to ask his secretary, Jia. She knew everything that was going on with my husband's work."

Fergus saw one of the guards check her watch. They didn't have long.

Alice noticed it too. "Mrs Zhu, we were looking through the evidence photographs yesterday. I was curious about the rug upon which your gun was found. Did you and your husband buy it for the flat?"

Charmian grimaced and the flicker of a sad smile played on her lips. "It was a running joke between us. We bought that flat partly because of the beautiful, natural wood floors. But within a few weeks of moving in, the management company informed us that the couple downstairs had repeatedly complained about the noise made by our footsteps on the wood. We ignored the letters for a while. We were far too busy to be concerned about that fussy, unreasonable old couple."

Alice nodded encouragingly.

"Then the head of housekeeping turned up with that hideous rug. She said it was complimentary from the management company and would cushion the noise whilst protecting the floor. It was like nothing Deming and I would usually buy – cheap and synthetic. But we kind of felt like it was a requirement that we keep it. The cleaners would have noticed if we hadn't and we certainly didn't want to get evicted or fined."

Alice nodded, "I understand."

Fergus said quickly, as the guards moved forward to flank their prisoner, "can you recall anything unusual that occurred between you and Deming in the weeks before the shooting – anything at all, however small or insignificant?"

Charmian seemed to be making a monumental effort to search her memory. "The only thing which comes to mind is that Deming was suddenly asking me about Scotland. In twenty odd years of marriage he'd never seemed particularly interested in my homeland, my background. I put it down to his age. That stage of life when you have more behind you than ahead. That's all I can think of, I'm sorry."

As the guards hustled her away, Fergus managed to reach across and shake Charmian's hand. He held onto it for as long as he could before she was led from the room.

Chapter 15

Dani opened the front door of her flat and was met with the sound of classic music. She smiled to herself as she kicked off her shoes and padded down the hallway to the kitchen.

James had his smart pad propped up against the bread bin. It was producing a background of melodious tunes whilst her partner prepared dinner. "It's Howell's new album," he called over to her.

"Very nice," Dani replied, picking up the device and turning down the volume. "Sorry, I just wanted to be able to talk."

James threw a handful of chopped peppers into a sizzling pan on the stove. "Sounds ominous."

She moved across and kissed his cheek. "It isn't. Just work."

James grabbed a bottle of wine and two glasses, ushering Dani towards the small kitchen table. "Feel free to share."

She smiled. "Andy's hunch has turned into a full-blown murder enquiry with a hard-core pornography racket thrown in."

"Trouble seems to follow that guy around," James added affectionately.

"DCS Douglas has just gone into theatre for root canal surgery and I've allowed Alice Mann indefinite leave to pursue a lost cause fighting the Chinese legal system."

"Ouch. On both scores." James took a mouthful of wine.

"Which leaves me desperately short of officers at

Pitt Street. Without Phil, I haven't got a single DI currently serving on my team."

"Has Andy taken the Inspector exams?"

"No, and the next batch aren't until June."

"Then you'll have to bring someone in. What do they call it – a secondment?"

Dani took a swig from her glass. "Yes, but when you're in the heat of a murder investigation, you need to be able to trust your officers. The teamwork is essential. It almost feels easier to take on the tasks ourselves, to ensure they're being completed correctly. There's so much arse-covering involved these days. I can't have some newbie making rookie mistakes."

James laughed. "Spoken like a true micro-manager. You can't run this case single-handed. At least bring in another DS to give Andy a hand. It sounds like one of those cases with a lot of grunt work. Sally is often defending men who've been found with illegal porn on their computers. We're talking hundreds of man-hours to sift through that filth."

Dani nodded dolefully, draining her glass. "That's true enough, although I'm dumping most of it on Vice."

James looked suddenly thoughtful. "You've worked on plenty of cases that have brought you into contact with other divisions. There must have been officers there who you thought were worth their salt. Couldn't you request someone specific? Then you'd already have a basis of trust."

Dani leant forward and kissed him deeply on the lips. "You know what? Sometimes I believe you're a total genius."

*

Andy was relieved that he knew the officer sitting in

the passenger seat beside him. Not particularly well, but their paths had crossed before in a favourable way.

DS Sharon Moffatt had pulled back her unruly blond curls in a ponytail at the base of her neck. She'd left her house in East Lothian in something of a hurry that morning after her boss called to say that DCI Bevan wanted to second her urgently to the Serious Crime Division. This was the kind of opportunity you grabbed with both hands.

Andy pulled the car up to the kerb, halfway along Clyde Street. He turned to his colleague. "Garfield's girlfriend is called Natalie Flynn. She's 32 years old and they were together for 8 years."

"He had a taste for younger women, then?" Sharon had been reading the case files closely.

"Aye, when I first came knocking, I thought she was the daughter."

Sharon nodded knowingly.

"Flynn works at a beauty salon on Cook Street. The manager confirms she's been in every day for the past month."

"Might she have taken a weekend to get to Mull and back. Perhaps the girlfriend knew about Garfield's retreat up there, or she followed him and got the surprise of her life."

Andy shook his head. "She works most Saturdays and never had two days on the trot to make the trip. I don't see her wielding a heavy industrial light either. She's a fragile wee thing."

"Okay," Sharon said breezily. "Just double checking."

Andy got out of the car and led the way to the front door. He liked Moffatt. She was certainly more on the ball than Dan Clifton.

Flynn opened up swiftly. She ushered the officers into the sitting room facing a neat garden.

Andy noticed that the little dog was tied up out there.

Flynn followed his gaze. "I've had to put poor Rusty out the back. The police being all over the house has really upset him."

"Cute dog," Sharon added.

"Thanks," Flynn replied, her narrow shoulders relaxing slightly. "He's all I've got now."

Andy shuffled forward in the seat. "We need to ask you some more questions, Miss Flynn."

"I thought you might."

"Did you realise that Kenneth Garfield hadn't been employed by Murray's Haulage since November of last year."

"No, I didn't."

"How do you know that the call you received from Kenneth three weeks ago, was made from the port of Harwich?"

"Because Ken told me, didn't he? And like a dozy idiot, I didn't realise he was feeding me a bunch of lies."

"We will need you to provide us with a list of dates when Kenneth was away from home, preferably covering the last twelve months."

Flynn looked overawed by the task. "I might still have last year's diary in the kitchen drawer. That should give me most of the dates. I always jotted down when he was away."

"That's great," Sharon added. Then her tone became softer, more sympathetic. "Natalie, I know our colleagues have told you about the types of obscene materials being produced in the place where Ken's body was found. I'm afraid we must ask if you were aware that Ken could have been involved in the production of such materials, or if he ever asked you to take part in the production of explicit or pornographic materials."

Natalie automatically pulled her cardigan more tightly around her tiny chest. "He tried to film us once. This was years ago. I told him it wasn't my cup of tea and he never asked again."

"He wanted to film the two of you having sex?" Sharon clarified.

The woman nodded.

"How old were you at this time?"

"Must have been about twenty-five. It wasn't long after we started going out."

"And Ken would have been, what? Late forties?" Andy added, as casually as he could.

"Yeah, something wrong with that?" Natalie looked indignant.

"Nothing at all," Sharon soothed. "My husband is older than me and we've had to shoulder some prejudice over the years."

Natalie shifted towards Sharon. "It was tough sometimes. People didn't always understand. But Ken and I loved each other, especially at the start."

The DS kept her tone conversational. "And how did you and Ken meet?"

Natalie blinked for a moment before saying, "he was a friend of my da's."

"And what's your Dad's name, Natalie?"

"Alan."

Andy cleared his throat and stood. "Thanks Miss Flynn, you've been most helpful."

The woman looked startled, as if she had certainly not intended to be.

*

Andy drove them back to Pitt Street. "She mentioned on my previous visit that her dad lived on the Crosshouse Estate. We can check out Alan Flynn on the database when we get back to the station. I've asked DC Clifton to sort you out a desk."

"Cheers." Sharon crinkled her pretty, rounded

face. "Who lets their twenty-five year old daughter date one of his sleazy, middle aged mates?"

"A dodgy bastard," Andy added. To his surprise, Sharon laughed heartily. He shifted round to catch her eye. "How does your husband feel about you trekking all the way over here to Glasgow for this case?"

Sharon's eyes twinkled with mischief. "I'm not married."

"But you told Natalie Flynn - ," Andy's words cut out as the penny dropped.

"I figured we needed to get her on side. Any information we give her in interview that's unrelated to the specifics of the case aren't admissible in court."

Andy turned his attention back to the road ahead, a wide grin on his face. He was going to enjoy working with Sharon Moffatt. She was his kind of gal.

Chapter 16

Fergus had insisted that Alice take the day to visit the Forbidden City. He felt guilty enough at dragging her half way around the world. She could at least see something of its treasures.

The lawyer had a meeting with some British officials at the UK embassy that morning. He took a cab from their hotel to Guanghua Road, where the embassy was situated. Fergus couldn't help but stare upwards through the back window of the taxi at the China World Trade Centre building, which seemed to loom up into the clouds. He'd never been into the bustling midst of the business district before.

The lobby of the embassy was cool and tranquil by comparison. Fergus was directed up a flight of stone steps to a marbled landing with tall ceilings and portraits on every wall. Two men in dark suits emerged from a door inset into an ornate panel. They guided him to a set of sofas overlooking the lobby below.

"Good morning, Mr Kelso. My name is David Acomb. I'm the First Secretary to the British Ambassador. This is Tom Weaver, my attaché."

Fergus shook their hands. "I was rather hoping to speak with Sir Arnold himself. My client's execution date has been brought forward. The situation has become very urgent."

Acomb nodded sombrely. "I'm afraid the Ambassador is in high level talks all this week. The PM is visiting China at the end of the month. We are hoping to secure good trade deals as a result of it."

"I'm sure she won't want reports of the execution

of a UK citizen to blight that tour," Fergus added dryly.

Acomb knitted his brow. "I've read through the court transcripts and the police reports very carefully, Mr Kelso. Charmian Zhu has dual citizenship. She has lived in China for over twenty years. The case against her would have satisfied any British judge." He sighed heavily. "I've come across many injustices during my time here in Beijing. In a couple of cases we've been able to help commute the sentence of British born prisoners accused of financial crimes – some of which also incur the death penalty. But in the case of Mrs Zhu, we couldn't risk insulting our Chinese hosts by intervening."

Fergus felt his hackles begin to rise. "I'm familiar with the case details, sir. I agree the evidence against the accused was strong. But if the case were being tried in the UK, we would have access to psychological and medical reports, more rigorous testing of the forensics. Most importantly, a guilty verdict would *not* result in death by firing squad." The lawyer realised his voice had risen. The attaché was glancing about them uncomfortably.

"No, that's correct," Acomb replied, equally forcefully. "But those are the laws of China. Your client agreed to operate within those laws when she chose to make her home here." His voice softened a little. "Look, Mr Kelso, diplomacy is a delicate skill. We know that the practices of our host country don't always comply with our own, but we must *respect* them. One of our strongest remits is not to interfere. Because imagine how we would feel about foreign countries passing judgement on the *British* legal system?"

"I shouldn't mind in the slightest," Fergus retorted, getting to his feet. "Are you sure this passive approach has nothing to do with our new PM being desperate to court international trade? We can't rock the boat now that we've cast off our European trading partners. Even if it means turning a blind eye to human rights violations?"

Acomb was on his feet now too. "I think you'd better leave, Mr Kelso. Before I decide to report your unprofessional conduct to your head of chambers back in Edinburgh."

Kelso let out a snort of disgust. "Don't worry. I've wasted enough time here already."

*

The offices of Asia Trust Management were within walking distance of the embassy. Fergus knew that the reception staff in these international companies usually spoke English. He just hoped that Deming's secretary did too.

Fergus was directed towards a waiting area by the tall glass windows facing the busy street. A woman was already seated on one of the angular sofas, flicking through an English copy of the China Daily.

He laid a hand on her shoulder. "I wasn't expecting to see you here."

Alice glanced up and smiled. "I did the whole tour, I promise. Then the tourist bus took us on a detour to view the skyscrapers. We passed the Asia Management building so I asked the driver to drop me off early…"

Fergus smiled ruefully. "You're a detective. I could hardly stop you from investigating. Especially as that's why I brought you here."

"Did you ask to see Jia?"

"Yes, how about you?"

"I've just been sitting here, watching people come

and go. Getting a feel for the place. I didn't want to tread on your toes."

"Tread away," he chuckled. "Stamp if you like. There's nobody else in this city who wants to help me."

"No luck with the consulate?"

Fergus shook his head. "The case is too delicate for the government to get involved in. Especially as *trade* takes priority right now."

"I can see that."

Whilst they were talking, a middle aged Chinese lady had approached them from the lifts. "Excuse me, you are Mr Kelso? You wanted to speak with me about Mr Zhu?"

Fergus turned around. "Jia?" he enquired.

"That's right. Would you like to come up to my office?"

*

The office floor was uncluttered but luxuriously furnished. Jia directed them to a small room which led away from a larger, conference area boasting an impressive view.

"Take a seat, please." Jia slipped behind her desk. "The company has not properly replaced Mr Zhu yet. For the time-being, I am handling his client list."

Alice thought she detected a catch in the woman's voice when she mentioned her old boss.

"Thank you for seeing us. You must be extremely busy," Fergus commented, with genuine gratitude.

"I was very devoted to Mr Zhu. What happened to him was a tremendous shock to his colleagues. I worked with Deming for over ten years. I know Charmian well too, although her name is not mentioned now amongst his remaining family and friends."

"Well, she's still around, but only just," Fergus added.

Jia nodded sadly. "Yes, I read that her sentence was to be carried out within weeks. That's why I wanted to speak with her lawyers. My interview with the police was very brief. I could have said more."

"Such as?" Alice prompted.

She sighed. "Mr and Mrs Zhu were married for many years. They loved each other. In my early working life, as a secretary to powerful businessmen, I was asked to book hotel rooms and buy gifts for mistresses. This was never the case with Deming."

"The local police weren't interested in this background information?"

"Why should they be? The police had the weapon and Charmian at the scene with her fingerprints all over it. That meant the case was closed."

"It's difficult to blame them," Alice muttered.

"Yes," agreed Jia. "But the context is always crucial. Facts can lie."

Alice was starting to wonder of the woman wasn't a little eccentric.

"Oh, there is nothing mystical about this," Jia continued. "It is just that the facts point to Charmian being a cold-blooded killer and one who would implicate herself in the process of committing murder. This is not the woman I know."

"Or the woman I have met," Fergus added.

Alice shuffled forward. "Charmian said her husband had secured an important client just before they took their holiday. She suggested you would know more details about this?"

Jia nodded. "Yes, I'm in the process of finalising the contracts right now. His name is Morgan Schrager. He is an American businessman who runs his Asian arm out of Kuala Lumpur. He has chosen

Asia Trust Management to handle his considerable investment portfolio. But it was Deming that he really warmed to. They met at a conference in Hong Kong last year. Schrager said he trusted Deming immediately, something the billionaire rarely did with anyone."

"But Schrager is still bringing his business to you, even now that Deming is dead?"

Jia looked sad. "Yes, he seems an honourable man. Schrager said he shook hands on the deal with Deming and he isn't going to go back on it now, especially in the tragic circumstances. But I suspect we'll have to prove ourselves worthy in the following months."

Fergus furrowed his brow. "Deming must have handled huge amounts of money for clients over the years. Have there ever been any major losses? Might your boss have made enemies out of clients who felt he lost their savings?"

"Deming was careful with his investments. He spread portfolios widely and absorbed losses into wider gains. This is why he was such a successful banker. Major clients wouldn't have brought their money to us otherwise. It is the younger, more rash traders who gamble with other people's money. We don't employ those types here."

Fergus nodded resignedly. "Well, there appears to be no motive for anyone in Deming's professional life to want him dead. This is bad news for Charmian."

Jia's face fell. "I suppose that is correct."

Alice tried one last question, "Deming's sister claimed that her brother was anxious about something in the final few weeks of his life. He hadn't gone into specifics, but Lui thought it was serious. Did you notice a change in his behaviour? You obviously worked very closely with him."

Jia considered this carefully. "Deming was a

reserved individual. He didn't share details of his personal life with me." She crinkled the pale skin around her dark eyes. "He asked me to dial through a couple of unusual international calls about a month before his death. Typically, I know the codes for Hong Kong, London and New York. This was different and Mr Zhu was cagey about the details. He gave me only a number, not a name or an agency as he would normally do. As soon as the line rang, I was to put him straight through, not speak to anyone myself."

"Do you have a note of the number?" Alice's interest had been piqued.

"I can get the number for you from our call records. It might take a couple of hours, though. But I can remember the international code. It stuck in my head because I'd not been required to dial it before. 0033."

Fergus got out his smartphone and looked the code up. He glanced at Alice before declaring, "Deming had been making calls to France just before his death. I wonder why he'd had cause to do that?"

Chapter 17

The Crosshouse Estate lay on the Southside of the river. Andy knew the area had slowly gentrified over the previous twenty odd years, as young professionals bought up the low-rise, ex-council properties when the city centre had priced them out.

The Flynns' property was probably one of the last to remain under council control. It possessed all of the original sixties fixtures and fittings, now oddly back in fashion. Janet Flynn looked very much like her daughter. Alan Flynn was thin and heavily lined, even for his sixty-two years. DS Clifton had found out that Alan had been a cook at the infirmary and was now retired. Janet was still a nurse there.

"You'll have heard about the murder of Kenneth Garfield up on Mull?" Andy said matter-of-factly.

Janet nodded. "Aye, we've had Natalie on the phone night and day, wondering if she's going to get turfed out of their flat."

"Your daughter informed us that Ken was a friend of yours, Mr Flynn – before the two of them became an item."

Flynn shrugged his thin shoulders. "I'm not sure you'd call it that. We both used to drink at the Brace of Pistols, over on Ballater Street, do you know it?"

Andy dipped his head. He knew it all too well.

"It turned out Ken had an interest in the horses, like me. He'd come over to the flat on big race days. That's when he first met Nat, I expect."

"Did Kenneth enjoy a flutter, then?" DS Moffett added casually.

Flynn creased his brow. "He didnae have a problem, if that's what you're driving at. He was just one of those fellers who spends his Saturday lunchtimes in the bar and the afternoons at the bookies. It's recreation, pure and simple."

Andy certainly knew it always started out that way. "And you were both happy for Kenneth to start courting your wee girl back then?"

Janet shuffled up in her seat defensively. "Natalie was twenty-five when she and Ken hooked up. She was hardly still a wee girl. He had a decent job and his own home. She could have done worse."

Alan let out a low grumble. "I wasnae happy at first, no. Ken was closer to my age than hers. In fact, I took him aside at the Brace of Pistols and told him to back off."

Janet turned sharply to look at her husband. "You never told me that."

"Aye, well. It was over soon enough. I gave him a shake, told the man to find someone his own age. But Ken crumpled, declared his love for our Nat. Promised to look after her and treat her right. So, I agreed to give him a chance."

"And that was eight years ago?" Sharon clarified.

"Aye, about that. For the first five year' he was definitely true to his word. But for the last few Ken was going AWOL for weeks at a time. We'd no idea he lost his job at the haulage yard. Christ knows what he was really up to."

"Does the name Robert Addison mean anything to you?"

Alan shifted his weight from one foot to the other. "I know Ken's body was found in his barn. Natalie told us. Before that, we'd never heard of him."

"What about Leonard Dalgleish? It looks like he and Ken were involved in a pornography business together."

Janet's body recoiled, as if she'd been physically struck.

"No, I'm not familiar with the names of these men. I told you, Ken was just someone from the pub, then he started stepping out with Nat." He rung his heavily veined hands. "We knew he was up to no good these last months. But I swear we had no idea he was peddling filth. I'd have had Nat straight out of that house if I'd known."

"When was the last time you saw Kenneth?"

"It was Boxing Day. He and Nat had a quiet Christmas together, but they came here for their tea on the 26th."

Tears were misting Janet's eyes. "The pair seemed happy together. There was no hint of anything like what you're suggesting. I know Ken was secretive, but what man isn't?"

Alan flinched almost imperceptibly at this comment. "We saw our daughter much more often than we saw him. To be honest, I think this may not be such a bad thing for Nat. She can meet someone her own age now, maybe have a few bairns before it's too late. I know that sounds callous. But family comes first."

"Aye, I understand what you're saying," Andy replied, thinking this was very likely the most honest statement the man had made since they arrived.

*

"What did you think of Flynn?" Sharon asked Andy, when they were back at his workstation.

"He was lying about something."

"Do you think it was about knowing Addison?"

"That could have been part of it. I'm certain the guy was hiding something that related to him and Kenneth. Perhaps they were more than just occasional drinking buddies."

Sharon nodded. "It might be worth checking out Garfield's fondness for the horses."

Andy swung his chair towards the pile of reports fanned out on his desk. "His bank account was pretty healthy. This was likely because of his income from the pornography business. But in my experience, folk with a gambling problem are always skint. They don't comfortably make their mortgage payments each month like Garfield did."

"Fair point."

DS Clifton approached the desk. "I've got the passenger manifests from Cal-Mac, sir."

"Good job, Dan. Anything of interest?"

Clifton tapped a name on one of the print-outs. "Kenneth Garfield was on the lunchtime ferry to Tobermory on Saturday the 5th. Roughly three weeks ago. He must have been staying on the island since he went missing from his place."

"And the *PM* report puts his death at last Friday evening, sometime before midnight. So, Garfield spent at least two weeks on Mull before he was killed."

"No other familiar names cropped up on the passenger lists, sir. According to the ferry records, Addison has been on the island for the last three months."

"But we all know those manifests aren't foolproof. It would have been possible for Addison to get on one of those crossings using a false name. Foot passengers never get checked."

"Aye, we've got officers from Highlands and Islands questioning ferry staff and passengers about possible sightings of Addison this weekend. We're assuming he'd try to leave on the Saturday or Sunday after the murder."

"Does the man have any notable features?"

Sharon asked doubtfully.

Andy handed her a blurry copy of Addison's photo-driving licence. An expressionless, pale, late-middle aged face, with a short crop of white hair stared out at them.

She squinted at it with a grimace. 'He could be any fifty-year old the length and breadth of the country."

Andy was forced to agree. "I can't imagine the man sticking in anyone's memory for long."

"Do you want me to suggest a new tack to the Highland division, sir?" Clifton enquired.

Andy sighed. "No, we need to make all the appropriate enquiries. Let's just hope we turn up another piece of evidence soon. Because what we've got so far is pretty bloody thin."

Chapter 18

The band playing in the YouTube video sounded tinny but reasonably good. Dani placed her tablet on the coffee table and they listened for a while, watching the amateur prancings of the middle-aged singer.

"So, that's Caroline Graham?"

James nodded. "I believe she had a music contract at some point. Caz produced a couple of albums but it didn't amount to much."

"And now she records sessions straight to YouTube?" Dani's voice was incredulous.

James chuckled. "Actually, if you have a look at the bottom of the screen, The Highland Wailers have nearly 200,000 subscribers. This is the way many artists get their work out to the public these days."

"She's not as successful as her ex-husband."

"No, that's true enough. But Howell was lucky to hit the big-time as a folk musician. It's extremely unusual."

Dani relaxed back against the cushions of her sofa. "After you gave me the name, I looked her up on the system. Caroline lives in Nairn with her husband."

"Howell told me she re-married. They've got two young children now."

"So, *Caz* moved on with her life better than Howell did."

James snuggled up beside her. "It's like you said, some folk manage to bounce back better than others. Caz's culpability was greater than Howell's, but she was able to forgive herself and move on. I bet she's a great mum now. Isn't that better than suffering forever for one mistake?" His voice was full of passion.

Dani glanced across at him. "Are we talking about Caz, or you?"

James turned and rested his hands on her shoulders. "I know I made a mistake. But I'm here to put it right. I'll spend my whole life making it up to you, if that's what it takes."

Dani leant forward and kissed his lips. "I'm not in the business of punishing anyone but criminals. Don't let your guilt about an error of judgement make you place yourself in the company of villains."

James sat back on the edge of the cushion, his arms still around Dani. "Do you believe Caz is a villain?"

The DCI narrowed her eyes. "She caused the death of her daughter, intentionally or not, and seems to display no real remorse. I'm sorry, James, but I'd have to say yes."

*

Fergus added the sheet of paper to the growing pile on his hotel bed. "We don't have the ability to trace the number."

"I could call my colleagues in Glasgow. If we have the permission of the Beijing police, they could find out which property in France the number is registered to," Alice explained.

Fergus shook his head, "I don't want to hand this over to the Chief of Police just yet. The evidence might implicate Charmian more."

Alice didn't think the burden of evidence could get any worse against their client, but she refrained from saying so. "Then our only option is to ring it."

Fergus sat very still on the edge of the bed. "I'm

not sure why, but I have a bad feeling about this."

Alice lay her hand on his. "Then let me make the call. I'm trained for this kind of thing."

"Okay, if you don't mind?"

"Of course I don't. I'm here in China to help."

Fergus got up and moved to the window whilst Alice called down to reception and requested an outside line to make an international call.

The wait whilst they were connected seemed interminable. Finally, Alice was able to punch in the row of numbers Jia had provided them with from the Asia Management phone records.

The line at the other end connected with a long, faint buzz. The voice that answered was croaky and distant. "Bonjour?"

"Bonjour, je m'appelle DS Alice Mann. Je suis une femme policier en Ecosse. Parlez vous anglais?"

There was a crackly silence at the other end for several moments. "En Ecosse?" the woman's voice finally answered.

"Oui, c'est vrai."

"Sorry, I'm so used to speaking French now. You took me by surprise. You are a policewoman from Scotland? Why are you calling us, what's happened?"

Alice could detect the woman's accent more clearly now. Her brain was ticking over fast, attempting to put the pieces together. "Mrs Wilson?" She ventured.

"Yes, of course it is. What do you want with us?"

"I'm in Beijing, Mrs Wilson. Your number came up in connection with our enquiries."

The line crackled noisily, but there was no reply.

"I'm part of the team working on your daughter's appeal. I'm really hoping that you and your husband may be able to help us. But we don't have much time."

Chapter 19

The pair had moved down to the hotel bar. Fergus ordered them both a gin and tonic.

He took a long sip. "Those were my grandparents."

Alice nodded. "Apparently, the Wilsons moved to a house in the Pay de la Loire when Colin retired over fifteen years ago. Anita says they hardly ever return to Perthshire now."

"I wasn't aware they'd retired to France. All I knew was that Charmian rarely saw her parents and hadn't been back to her hometown in over a decade."

Alice tried a mouthful of the ice-cold drink. It was incredibly refreshing. "I got the feeling the couple are largely estranged from their daughter. Anita admitted she was aware of Charmian's sentence, but she said no one in their village knew anything about it. The Wilsons had simply denied to themselves what was happening."

Fergus shook his head. "How could they abandon their own child like that? Just when she needs them most?" The man seemed to suddenly realise the irony of his words. He drove his fist down hard onto his thigh. "Alice, have I been a class 'A' fool? Charmian abandoned me as a baby and her parents are just as morally weak. Why on earth am I fighting for them?"

Alice leant forward and squeezed his hand. "Because you're better than they are. Besides, there's more to this. I asked Anita why her son-in-law had been calling them before his death."

Fergus tilted his head to one side, still curious.

"She said they barely knew Deming. Whenever Charmian had visited the pair in Scotland, she was alone. The calls from him came from out of the blue. Deming told them he was planning a big 50th birthday bash for his wife. He wanted lots of family and friends to come. He needed names and addresses of Charmian's old contacts and school mates."

"That doesn't sound like the actions of a man in an unhappy marriage."

"No, but it doesn't sound much like the Zhus either. Charmian and Deming were reserved and private people. Charmian barely wanted to see her parents, let alone the folk she sat next to in primary four."

Fergus nodded slowly, his brow knitting. "You don't believe there was going to be a party?"

"No, I don't. I think Deming was investigating his wife. He was finding out as much as he could about her past. His starting point was to get as much information as possible out of the Wilsons. Then he could interview others from her life back in Scotland. Before she met him."

Fergus finished off his gin in one gulp. "Then I was right," he declared. "This evidence doesn't look good for Charmian. Not good at all."

*

Alice glanced through her messages. DCI Bevan had informed her that an officer from City and Borders had been brought in to assist Calder with his murder inquiry. She felt guilty and a little disappointed. It was tough to imagine someone taking on her role in her absence. But Bevan's tone was encouraging, asking Alice to keep her updated with developments.

Fergus emerged from the bathroom, towel drying his thick, dark hair. "Are you okay?" He immediately enquired, obviously noting her downcast expression.

"Yeah, fine. I got a text from Bevan. In the pornography case we were handling back in Glasgow a body has turned up. They've had to second more officers."

Fergus sat beside her on the bed and pulled her into his arms. "If you want to go back, I completely understand. You've helped me so much already."

She shook her head. "No, we're just beginning to get somewhere here. If we need to start investigating Charmian's life in Scotland then I'm the best person to do that."

Fergus swept a stray hair away from her forehead. He kissed her face and then her mouth. Alice slipped her hand underneath the robe to touch his warm, slightly damp skin. They fell back together onto the sheets and made love until falling into a deep, untroubled sleep.

Alice wasn't sure what time it was when she woke. They hadn't pulled across the thick curtains and the sky outside was a purplish black. The ubiquitous lights of the city made the contours of the hotel room just about visible.

There was an unfamiliar shadow at the end of the double bed. Alice's body stiffened with fear. She could hear Fergus's steady breathing beside her and knew he was still asleep.

The shadow suddenly shifted to the lawyer's side of the bed. She could make out the artificial bulk of a dark padded jacket. The only thing the DI could think to do was to let out a long, piercing scream.

She could hear voices in nearby rooms and the sounds of footfalls along the corridor outside. The figure paused for a moment and then made a dash for the door.

Alice grabbed on her nightshirt and bottoms. Fergus was awake now too and bombarding her with questions. She ignored him and followed the intruder's escape route into the corridor. People were standing outside their rooms in nightgowns looking drowsy and perplexed. For once in her life, Alice desperately wished she knew some Chinese. Where did he go? She wanted to shout. But the man in the dark padded jacket and balaclava was nowhere to be seen. He was by now in one of the lifts perhaps, or halfway down a tradesman's staircase. She had no hope of being able to catch up with him.

Chapter 20

Len Dalgleish looked grubby. Not necessarily because he hadn't washed. He just had that kind of stubbly growth of grey sprinkled hair on his chin that made DS Moffatt think of dirty old men with top shelf magazines stuffed under their single beds.

He was also uncooperative. Andy was trying hard not to lose his cool. "You admit to knowing the deceased, Kenneth Garfield?"

"Aye, we served together in Belfast."

Andy leant forward. "Don't you think it's a coincidence that your old army pal was found murdered in a pornography studio not unlike the one you operated from your house?"

"I don't want to comment on that. My lawyer told me not to."

Andy felt his hackles rise. "The Fiscal's office have enough to charge you with producing and distributing extreme pornographic material. That carries a maximum 5 year sentence. Are you seriously prepared to carry the can for this operation alone?"

Len appeared to be considering this. "Robbie was in charge," he finally declared.

Andy and Sharon weren't expecting this. They exchanged glances.

"You mean Robert Addison?" Andy clarified.

"Aye, Robbie was with us at Girdwood Barracks until '85. That's when he left the forces. But he got back in touch maybe four years later. He recalled we all shared similar *tastes*."

"And it was Addison who suggested you make a

business out of those *tastes*?"

Len nodded. "Robbie had come into some cash. His old Grandad had died, leaving him the farm on Mull. There were plenty of outhouses on the land that no one ever visited. We started out there, paying the local tarts to get their taps 'aff for the camera."

"But the business built over the years."

"We sold photos to start with, to dirty mags and dirty old men we knew down the pub. Then the internet came along and turned our little venture global."

Moffatt inwardly sighed. The World Wide Web was a goldmine to these creeps.

"Is that when you set up the studio in your front-room?"

Len's posture became defensive. He folded his arms across his chest. "Robbie told me to do that. He gave me all my instructions. I never gave up the day job. The photography was just a hobby for me, a way to earn extra beer money."

Andy nearly let out a grunt of disgust. "We've got photos of you with the girls you exploited for this *beer money.* Most of them eastern Europeans desperate for cash. You don't look particularly unwilling in them. When the jury take a look at your video collection, I can't imagine them warming to your argument of coercion."

"Wait till you see what Robbie was producing."

Andy took a deep breath. "When did you last see Addison?"

"We communicated online, using false names and that. It's been about a month since I sent him some new material."

"What about Garfield, when did you see him?"

"Ken was a small-time player. He used to come around to my place and help me with the technical stuff. But I'd not set eyes on him since before

Christmas. If he was hanging around Robbie's place on Mull, then he must have been doing some jobs for him."

"Do you believe that Robert Addison killed Kenneth Garfield? Perhaps with you in prison, Addison was worried Garfield might implicate him in the porno ring."

"I dunno. Robbie's definitely capable of it. Ken probably pissed him off by asking for money to keep quiet. He was always an idiot, in out of his depth."

Andy nodded. "If Addison were on the run from the police, do you know where he might go?"

Len shrugged. "Robbie did a lot of different jobs after he left the regiment. He moved from place to place until his Grandad carked it. To be honest, he could be hiding anywhere." The man shifted forward. "I've helped you out now, yeah? You're gonna put in a word for me with the Fiscal?"

Andy felt his top lip involuntarily curl up. "I'll provide them with a transcript of the interview."

Len looked triumphant.

Andy eyed the man before them carefully. "What happened to you, Len? You were a soldier - man and boy, loyal to your regiment, serving your country in Northern Ireland during the worst of the troubles. What made you resort to churning out filth on the net? I believe there was a chance for you once – someone who loved you, who could have set you on a different path. Whatever happened to Karla?"

Len blinked vigorously, but his face showed no signs of emotion. "Oh, Karla would never have helped. You've got that quite wrong. In fact, I was actually a decent guy before I met her."

*

"Do you believe Dalgleish when he says Addison was the brains behind the operation?" Sharon asked, as she gratefully received the coffee that Dan Clifton had made for them.

"It makes sense. The farm in Mull was clearly the centre of the business. The records check out that Addison inherited the place in early '91."

"And the connection between the men was the time they spent serving together at Girdwood Barracks?" Dan clarified.

"Aye, it would seem so." Andy sipped his strong coffee. It was good.

"So, we're looking to charge Addison for the murder of Garfield and the running of the porn business," Sharon added, thinking out loud.

"Yes, but is it really likely there were only the two of them?" Dan interjected. "It sounds like Garfield wasn't one of the main players, but he certainly knew what was going on. Then we've got Dalgleish and Addison. Were there any other names that cropped up on the list you were given by the regiment, sir?"

Andy shook his head. "Those were the only three whose ages and service records matched up."

Sharon put down her cup. "What about this old girlfriend, Karla? Dalgleish seemed to be implicating her, too. What if we're looking at a woman being involved in all this?"

It went against Andy's instincts in cases like this, to imagine a woman could be capable of facilitating such nasty sexual exploitation. But the DS knew he needed to keep an open mind. "You're right Sharon. It's something we definitely need to consider."

Chapter 21

The thing that struck Alice most about the Beijing city police department, was how high tech it was. There were clearly no funding issues here.

She and Fergus were seated at the desk of Captain Chen. Seemingly the senior detective with the best grasp of English in the building. He had taken a preliminary statement from them and was now in discussion with his colleagues.

Alice turned to glance down the corridor, visible through a glass partition, as a tall man in a pin-stripe suit approached the office they were in.

Fergus followed her gaze. "That's Tim Weaver, attaché to the First Secretary. That's obviously all the embassy felt I warranted."

Weaver gave a perfunctory knock before entering. "Good morning Mr Kelso, DI Mann. I bring the Ambassador's deepest sympathies for your unpleasant ordeal."

Fergus waved away his comments. "Have you spoken to the Chief of Police? Has the intruder been found?"

Weaver shook his head. "Chinese officers were at the Imperial Hotel in minutes. But this man had already made his escape. They have patrol cars out searching for him now."

"How did he get past the security desk? How did he get into our room unnoticed, for heaven's sake?" Alice added.

"It seems the man took a security key from the pocket of a jacket hanging in the staff common room. It hadn't been locked for the night. The manager is dealing with the person responsible."

"It's easy enough to get into those rooms anyway," Fergus lamented. "I just want to know why he targeted us in particular. No other rooms were broken into tonight, I gather?"

Weaver creased his brow in concern. "I believe you were the only unfortunate victims of this thief."

Alice felt her frustrations rise. "Why do you think this was a robbery? Nothing was taken from the room. I saw the man, he went straight for Fergus. If I hadn't screamed, I don't know what he would have done."

Weaver clasped his hands together, a gesture designed to make his words sound more reasonable. "Captain Chen is working on the assumption that the thief was making for the bedside table of Mr Kelso. This is where guests typically keep their wallets, mobile phones and watches. When you woke up, DI Mann, he was interrupted in his robbery and fled."

"I want to speak with the Chief of Police. He was very helpful the last time I was in Beijing."

A muscle twitched under Weaver's right eye. "I can't allow you to do that, sir. This is a case of petty burglary and doesn't warrant being made into a full blown diplomatic incident. Captain Chen is dealing with the investigation very competently. I realise this intrusion was a shock, but no harm was done."

Alice got to her feet. "Can we be sure that this attack on Fergus has nothing to do with our work on Mrs Zhu's appeal? That hotel must have over 300 rooms. Why on earth did they target us?"

Weaver kept his voice level. "Chen checked the guest register. You were the only British couple staying in the establishment. He assumes the thief believed you to be wealthy visitors. It is possible this man is an employee at the hotel, or has connections to someone who is. Chen is investigating extremely thoroughly. Tourism is important to this city. The authorities want visitors to feel safe."

"But we aren't tourists," Fergus added dryly.

"No, but a petty thief would have no reason to know this," Weaver replied, his patience obviously running thin.

"I think that's rather the point, isn't it?" Alice commented, more to herself than anyone else. It was clear the consulate weren't going to be of any assistance to them. This was something they'd have to investigate for themselves.

*

The next hotel they chose was in a quiet suburb. They booked in under a false name, just to be sure. Alice preferred it. The building was more in the traditional Chinese style. Their room was on the ground floor and had access to a shared garden where mountains were just visible beyond the hedged boundary. The room even had a desk where they could lay out their evidence.

"Do you really believe that man wanted to kill me?" Fergus put his arm around Alice's waist as she stood beside him at the desk.

"My handbag was at the end of the bed. He showed no interest in it. I got the sense he'd been watching us for a few minutes while we were both asleep. When he worked out which side you were on, he moved straight towards you."

Fergus shuddered. "Thank God you screamed."

"His movements were silent and precise. It has the feel of a professional hit."

"*Why* would someone want to kill me?"

"I assume you've pissed somebody off with your

digging into Deming's murder. It must be a person who is powerful and well-connected. The job was carefully planned. The hit-man knew where to find the security card for the lock and could access the guest register for our room number."

"Does this person want us to stop appealing Charmian's death sentence, or stop investigating Deming's murder?"

Alice shrugged. "It's difficult to know. We never made it a secret we were staying at the Imperial Hotel. Our investigations around the city must have made us conspicuous. We need to be far more circumspect now."

Fergus frowned. "This attempt on my life came not long after we made that call to the Wilsons in France. You placed the call through the hotel switchboard. Do you think that was the trigger?"

Alice nodded slowly. "You could be right. The people who put out the hit obviously have accomplices at the hotel."

"Then that's where I think we should concentrate our efforts; on understanding the significance of the phone calls Deming made to France. We need to find out what Deming was so interested in from Charmian's past life."

"Yes, I agree. I'm just not entirely sure how we can do that from here."

Chapter 22

It was a crisp, sunny morning in Oban. The town had long been dominated by its port, which served the majority of the western isles.

Andy had received a call from the Highland Division in the early hours. DS Moffett didn't have time to get herself to Glasgow to accompany him, so DCI Bevan had volunteered herself. Driving through the Trossachs National Park with the boss beside him, felt like old times.

They pulled up outside the ferry terminal building as soon as they arrived. A burly man in a rain jacket moved forward to greet them.

"Morning, Ma'am. I'm DI Harper from Highlands and Islands."

"What have you got for us?" Dani asked matter-of-factly.

He led them past the passenger lounge to a large wooden jetty. The tide was high and lapping up at them on both sides. A tent had been erected halfway along, which was bending fiercely in the strong sea breeze. Underneath, the Glasgow detectives could make out a sheet of tarpaulin weighted down at the corners with bricks.

"The final ferry from Mull last evening was reporting a problem with its rear propeller. It was sluggish and causing the engine to lose power. The engineer took a closer look as soon as they got into port." Harper scratched his balding pate. "Turned out there was an obstruction in the mechanism, Ma'am."

Calder cleared his throat. "A *human* obstruction?"

"Aye, the remains of a body. The cadaver must have been floating in the water and got sucked into the propeller somewhere off the coast of Tobermory. There wasn't a great deal of it left. Whatever the techs managed to extract is under that sheet. The rest is a case for forensics."

Dani was extremely reluctant to look for herself. "Is there anything left that could identify the body, DI Harper?"

"The techs put all the solid objects in a bag. They'll need to go off for analysis." Harper sighed. "Off the record, Ma'am, our pathologist reckons it's the body of a male, probably middle-aged, taller than average due to the length of the femur. But all of this will go into the report."

Dani glanced at her colleague. "Robert Addison?"

Andy nodded. "Sounds like it. We'll need to test for his DNA. We should be able to track down a relative somewhere."

"So, you think this poor sod is the guy we've been looking for in connection with the murder of Kenneth Garfield?" Harper added.

"Yes, I suspect so."

"Do we think he murdered Garfield and then drowned himself in the sea?"

Dani frowned. "We'll need to know exactly how long he's been in the water to determine that. But I've got a gut feeling we're looking for a third person here."

"Somebody who was also at Addison's farm, Ma'am?" Andy commented.

She nodded. "You said there was a possibility more people were involved in this pornography ring than just Dalgleish, Garfield and Addison. If it turns out Addison was murdered too, then you're probably quite right."

Dani hadn't been to Mull since she was a little girl and her father had taken them on a trip to Fingal's Cave on Staffa, which lay off the west coast of the island. Addison's farm was considerably less appealing as a destination.

A dark farmhouse sat behind overgrown hedges up a steep drive from the coast road. The sheds and barns were dotted about within the shadowy canopy of the forest.

Andy strode past the main house. "We lifted dozens of prints from all over the property but none matched with anyone on our database. Not even Dalgleish."

"He told you he'd not been here for the best part of twenty years," Dani replied, following her DS to the first of the barns which was sealed off with police tape.

Andy lifted the cordon and pushed open the wooden doors. "Most of the cameras and equipment have been taken away by Vice. The sheets and clothing were also removed for analysis."

What remained were the rusty metal structures of several double beds, a series of gaudily framed mirrors, hung on almost every wall and suspended from wooden beams criss-crossing the roof.

"It looks pretty pathetic now," Dani commented.

"Vice sent us a summary of the contents of the tapes the local plods found. Most of them were a good decade old, their officers reckon that Addison was streaming to a live feed more recently, that way these scumbags can cover their tracks better."

"Was the material any worse than that lifted from Dalgleish's place?"

"Not really, Ma'am. It was just being produced on a larger scale here. Vice are fairly certain Addison had associates who brought the girls over to the island hidden in vans and cars. The Mull ferry doesn't perform very vigorous searches at either port. The farm doesn't have any near neighbours who might have reported the unusual activity."

"So, that's how the girls were brought in and out." Dani glanced about her. "Do we think the porn operation was linked to people trafficking?"

Andy nodded solemnly. "Yes, I'd bet money on it. Addison must have been working with some very nasty individuals."

"When Dalgleish was arrested, these men decided he might start talking, which prompted them to cover over the traces?"

"Dalgleish's only contacts were Addison and Garfield. Murdering them would leave us with no further witnesses."

"Sadly, they may be right. The traffickers could have disappeared straight back to eastern Europe after murdering Addison and Garfield. We don't have their prints or DNA on file. The killers may prove to be entirely invisible to us."

Andy shrugged his shoulders. "I've passed all the information that our Highland and Island colleagues have picked up from analysing the corpse to Vice. They're used to liaising with Interpol to track down perps. We haven't given up hope just yet."

Dani wasn't so sure she hadn't done just that. The barn had been fitted with several mains water taps. One of them had a hose attached to it. Empty bottles of bleach and cleaning fluids were scattered about the concrete floor. "I'm not convinced we're going to find much forensic evidence in this place."

Andy caught his boss's eye. "We've not yet dismissed the idea that Dalgleish had more associates here in Scotland. DS Moffett is convinced this Karla woman is involved somewhere along the line."

"Then concentrate on finding her. We need to nail at least one of these creeps with more than just pornography charges. Two men have met violent deaths and countless young girls have been trafficked and abused."

"Aye, you're right. There's not much more we can find out here. Let's get straight back to Glasgow."

Chapter 23

A trip back to the Asia Trust Management offices and an appointment with Jia had given Fergus access to Deming Zhu's papers and files for a brief period of time. Zhu's secretary didn't feel comfortable allowing a stranger to take them away, but permitted him to seek the specific information he wanted.

Jia told him her bosses weren't interested in keeping the contents of Deming's office, so she'd been gradually filling boxes, in the hope someone from his family would want it.

Fergus was very grateful there were still some effects left. The local police hadn't been interested in Deming's work papers. His professional life didn't seem to them to be connected to their case against Charmian in any way.

The Scottish lawyer sifted swiftly and efficiently through the material. He knew exactly what he was looking for. He and Alice had decided that anything Deming had written down regarding his investigation into his wife would have been kept here at his office, not in the flat he and Charmian shared.

It didn't take long for Fergus to find a notebook, along with a desk diary for the previous year, which listed names, phone numbers and addresses that he recognised as Scottish. Everything else was written in a language and script he simply couldn't decipher. Despite the generous way that Jia had assisted them, Fergus feigned disinterest in the items. Then when the secretary left the office for a few moments to speak with a colleague, he stuffed the books into his back pocket. Since the attempt on his life at the hotel, Fergus had shed some of his usual scruples.

Alice found a café local to their accommodation which sold fragrant teas in tiny cups and seemed to be off the usual tourist trails. They both sipped their drinks whilst flicking through Deming's notebooks.

"It would be difficult to prove he wasn't simply planning a big party," Fergus said despondently.

"Yes, but there's no way he'd be intending to invite all these folk listed here to come to Beijing. That's the kind of expense and hassle you'd only expect from immediate family members."

"Unless Deming was going to pay to bring them all over."

Alice frowned. "It's possible, but I still don't see it." She turned the notebook round and pointed to a particular entry, "This man is identified as 'Godfather'. I'm assuming that's to Charmian."

Fergus looked closely at the name. "Jeffrey Dalry. The address is in Pitlochry."

"Most of the addresses are in Perthshire. I could call one of my colleagues and get them to run the names through our databases, see if something interesting comes up. It might narrow our search."

Fergus finished his tea and took a deep breath. "I thought your division were in the middle of a multiple murder enquiry? You can hardly ask them to do our legwork for us."

"Well, I've got plenty of pals at the Pitt Street Station. I'm sure someone would do the checks for us, maybe during a lunchbreak."

Fergus shook his head. "No, I don't want you to ask for their help."

Alice looked puzzled. "Then what are you suggesting? This is our strongest lead."

Fergus leant forward. "I want you to go back to Scotland and investigate it for yourself." He reached out and laid his hand over hers. "Ever since that maniac broke into our hotel room I've not been comfortable. I asked you to come here with me, but I never had the slightest idea it would be dangerous. It's time for you to go home."

"What about you? That nutcase was out to silence *you*, not me. Beijing isn't a safe place for you to stay, either."

Fergus sighed deeply. "I have to be here, close to Charmian. Plus, there are some more leads in China I need to chase up. I hope you understand."

Alice did understand, but it hadn't stopped the tears from pooling in her eyes.

Chapter 24

Andy had been re-examining Len Dalgleish's personal effects. He'd taken out the correspondence from his one-time girlfriend, Karla, and made copies of the letters.

It was in an exchange of April 1989 that Karla mentioned a holiday they were planning to take to Normandy. She referred to a hotel in Honfleur and the dates they'd booked to stay; from the 6th to the 13th May. There was also a reference to a P&O ferry booking for early in the morning of Saturday 6th May, setting sail from Dover.

Karla's words were full of anticipation for this trip. She added that they would discuss the arrangements further at a future lunch date with her parents, whom she didn't name. But Karla did check that the venue was acceptable to Len and mentioned somewhere called, 'The Limes'.

Andy wondered if it was worth questioning Dalgleish again about this woman. He quickly decided it wasn't. If the man's solicitor was even vaguely worth his salt he'd object on the grounds there was no discernible connection to their current investigation.

The DS glanced over at Sharon. She was still working through the forensic evidence they'd been sent by the tech lab. "Have we got a time of death from the corpse yet?"

Sharon glanced up. "The *PM* indicated serious deterioration of the body in the water. The temperature was freezing, which made a time of death impossible to pin-point."

"Dammit."

"But the pathologist reckons from the extent of decay, our man went into the Firth of Lorn over a week ago."

"*Before* Ken Galbraith was murdered?"

"The evidence wouldn't stand up in court, but the doc reckons yes, it was before Galbraith met his fate, or certainly around a similar time, no later."

"What about an identification?"

"Due to the length of time the body was in the water, the lab couldn't extract much DNA, but they have got a useable sample. There were also a number of solid items attached to parts of the cadaver, including a watch. It had a silver casing and appeared to have been given to the owner on their retirement."

"How could they tell?"

Sharon pushed across a photograph of the item, taken by the technicians. "There's an engraving in the silver on the back. The initials R.A and the inscription '5th Scots Guards, 1986'."

"Well, the date fits with when Dalgleish claimed Addison left the forces." Andy sighed. "So, we can be fairly sure the body is Robbie Addison's?"

"As sure as you can ever be with a corpse that badly degraded. If we track down a family member willing to supply a swab for DNA comparison, we can make absolutely certain. We were lucky the body got entangled in the boat. It could have ended up out in the north Atlantic somewhere. Then we'd have been indefinitely chasing a dead man."

"Aye, it's good to know we've had luck in one area of this case."

Sharon dipped her head in the direction of the letters spread out on Andy's desk. "Any joy with our Karla character?"

"She talks about a holiday they were planning to take to northern France in '89. The letters stop after that, but I wonder if they actually took the trip. Do the ferry companies keep records going that far back?" "Well, we can only call them up and see."

*

Fortunately, P&O kept detailed passenger records on their databases, which stretched back decades. This was largely at the request of the Home Office and Customs and Excise. The channel tunnel hadn't opened until 1994, which was when the process became extremely rigorously monitored. But even in '89, Andy found that fairly detailed lists had been compiled.

In fact, due to the Lockerbie disaster of December the previous year, security at all ports and airports was stepped up. Andy remembered it well, even though he was just a teenager back then. His parents had friends in the town. The act of terrorism had shocked the nation.

The stark contrast between the procedures at Dover and Oban made him raise an eyebrow. But he supposed they *were* talking about a national border.

"I've been sent a list from passport control in addition to the booking register from the ferry company." Andy placed the print-out under Sharon's nose. He tapped a name highlighted with a neon marker. "There's Leonard Dalgleish. He boarded the 8.15 am crossing to Calais. His vehicle was listed as a Ford Transit."

"He didn't have a woman with him?"

"Nope. There's no Karla listed as a passenger that day."

Sharon creased her forehead. "That's odd. Why take a van? And if they'd planned the holiday together, even if the pair had split up subsequently, it seems odd Dalgleish went on his own. He didn't strike me as the type to enjoy French culture."

Andy's face was set in a grim line. "No, he certainly didn't. I tried the hotel Karla mentioned in her letter. It no longer exists."

"What are you thinking?"

"That maybe Dalgleish was always mixing business with pleasure on this trip. By the late 80s, Addison was cranking up his porn enterprise. Perhaps Dalgleish was taking some material to the continent. Or perhaps planning to bring something back."

"Some of the girls, you mean? In the back of his van would be risky, even in those old days when not every vehicle was given the once-over."

"He'd never have managed it with Karla in tow anyway. Her letters suggest she thought it was a romantic getaway." Andy ran a hand through his sandy hair, now not as thick as it once was. "But travelling as a couple would certainly have diverted the attention of the customs officials. I know how they operate. *Single* guys driving vans are their top priority."

"But Karla never accompanied him in the end."

Andy nodded slowly. "Aye, that's right. Maybe she discovered what Len was up to on the side and dropped him like a hot brick."

"Yeah, perhaps." Sharon's eyes were drawn back to the passenger lists. Her body stiffened. "Hey, did you see this entry, towards the bottom of the second page?"

Andy frowned. "What is it?"

Sharon ran a finger under the line of names, reading aloud, "Alan and Janet Flynn, plus one child under ten. Driving a Ford Sierra 1.6."

Andy let out a gasp. "Let me look at that!"

Sharon passed him the sheet.

"Bloody hell. What were the Flynns doing on the same ferry as Dalgleish? There's no flaming way that's a coincidence."

Chapter 25

Dani addressed the team from Andy's desk. "We've got two dead men – Garfield and Addison. Both of whom were murdered on Mull, the attacker as yet unidentified. Dalgleish was their business associate. He's on remand at Barlinnie for the foreseeable future. DS Calder, can you provide us with an update?"

Andy stood. "Of course, Ma'am. Thanks to the eagle eye of DS Moffett we now have a connection between the Flynns and Len Dalgleish. Ken Garfield was in a relationship with Alan Flynn's daughter, Natalie. Flynn was an old drinking pal of Garfield, but when interviewed, he claimed to know nothing about Dalgleish, Addison, or their nasty porno business." He scratched his head. "But when we chased up the whereabouts of Dalgleish's ex-girlfriend Karla, it led us to a ferry crossing made by Len in the May of 1989 to Calais. Sharon spotted that the Flynns were on that same ferry."

Dani shook her head in puzzlement. "What does this mean? Flynn wasn't in the army with the others, was he?"

"No, he was a cook at the infirmary for over a decade. But his age matches. Flynn is only a few years older than the rest of them."

"Then I suggest you concentrate on Alan Flynn. Go back and have another word. If he proves uncooperative, bring the man in," Dani suggested.

DC Clifton raised his hand. "They have cooks in the army too, don't they?"

Dani looked at him in mild surprise, a smile slowly forming on her face. "Yes they do, DC Clifton. They certainly bloody do."

*

The weather had brightened up when they returned to the Crosshouse Estate. Janet Flynn had the back door open onto a tiny balcony overlooking the quad. Her husband sat in a frayed armchair facing the sun, the daily newspaper lying unread on his lap.

"Would you like a cuppa?" The woman asked. "Is there any update on Ken's killer? We saw on the news they'd pulled a body out of the Lorn?"

"No thanks," Andy responded brusquely, ignoring her other comments. "It's your husband we've come to see."

Flynn barely shifted his gaze. "Oh, aye. What can I do for youse today?"

Andy perched on the arm of the sofa opposite him. "When we questioned you previously, we asked if you knew Len Dalgleish and Robert Addison. You claimed you didn't."

The man remained very still, continuing to stare out of the window.

"What's all this about?" Janet declared.

"Could we have that cup of tea now, Janet?" Sharon suggested. "I'll come and help you make it."

"You never told us that before you were a cook at the Glasgow Infirmary, you were a member of the Army Catering Corps from 1973 to 1988."

"You never asked." Flynn finally turned to look at Calder.

"And between '77 and '84 you were stationed at the Girdwood Barracks in Belfast, a period that coincided with Dalgleish, Addison and Garfield being soldiers there."

Flynn was silent.

"You must have known one another, you made their dinners for seven years for pity's sake." Andy leant forward. "Why did you take a trip to France in the May of 1989? Dalgleish travelled over on the same crossing. What were you doing there together?"

Flynn clearly wasn't expecting this question. His body stiffened. "That was decades ago. Why are you interested in that?"

Janet re-entered the room with a tray full of steaming mugs. "Why are you asking about our holiday to France in '89?" she cast a desperate glance at her husband, who was obstinately avoiding her eye. "It was Nat's first trip abroad. We stayed in a boarding house on the south coast of England after the first day of driving. Then we caught a ferry nice and early on the Saturday."

Calder shifted in her direction. "Where did you stay in France that holiday, Mrs Flynn?" He enquired innocently.

Her face instantly brightened at the memory. "Well, we were planning to head south and camp when the weather got warmer. But it was such a hot summer, we didn't need to go far, which was just as well, because Nat didn't enjoy car journeys at that age."

Alan Flynn swivelled almost 180 degrees in his chair. "Will you shut up, woman!" He growled. "Stop your stupid blethering!"

Janet looked shocked. Sharon slipped her hands under the heavy tray before the woman dropped it.

Flynn twisted towards Calder. "I'm saying nothin' until I have a lawyer present."

Andy nodded. "That's fine, sir. But the next time we talk, it will be at the Pitt Street police station."

Chapter 26

The flat felt strangely chilly and inhospitable. Alice turned the thermostat up before making a start on the unpacking. She supposed her flatmate had stayed over at her boyfriend's place the night before. The heating probably hadn't been on for a few days.

Alice was also tired after the long flight, this always made her feel cold. It was only just over a week since she'd last been at her Glasgow residence, but it felt like a lifetime. So much had shifted in such a short period.

A glance at the phone indicated there were no messages. Alice's heart sank. She'd vaguely hoped that DCI Bevan, or even Calder, would have been updating her on their current case. The detective padded into her bedroom and gave a wry smile. She'd inflated her own importance. Of course they hadn't. The pace of a murder investigation was intense. You barely had time to exchange pleasantries with your own loved ones, let alone a colleague who'd left the team in the lurch.

Now she was five thousand miles away, back in this familiar environment, Alice wondered at the madness of Fergus's mission. A foreign government; one with a shady human rights record and notoriously secretive criminal justice system was planning to execute a woman convicted of a capital crime. What hope did they have of stalling the process? Even the British Embassy was against them.

Alice tried to empty her mind. She stepped out of her grubby travelling clothes and into a hot shower. The young detective needed a straight nine hours of sleep before considering the situation any further.

*

Alice squared it with DCI Bevan before she ran the names on Deming Zhu's list through the police database software on her laptop. Charmian was a Scottish national and her appeal was still open. The DCI felt it was within their jurisdiction to investigate.

It was Jeffrey Dalry's name that had caught her attention. As Charmian's godfather, it seemed as if he would possess the greatest insight into the family's background history.

Dalry was 88 years old. He appeared to still be living in his own property in Pitlochry. A Google search informed Alice that Dalry was an ordained priest. His ministry had been at a small Roman Catholic church near the banks of Loch Faskally. The detective considered the possibility the Wilson family had been practicing Catholics.

She flicked to the page in Deming's notebook that held Dalry's number and proceeded to dial.

The phone seemed to be ringing for a very long time at the other end. Finally, a voice crackled onto the line.

"Hello?"

"Hello, Mr Dalry? This is DI Alice Mann from Police Scotland. I wondered if I might ask you a few questions?"

"Oh, of course Inspector. What is this regarding?"

"Were you aware that your god-daughter, Charmian Zhu, neé Wilson, had been arrested in Beijing?"

"Erm, yes, her parents called me with the news. It was a great shock, they were seeking comfort." His voice had become hesitant and wary.

"I have just returned from China. I've been helping the appeal team with their investigation. It appears Charmian's husband had your details in his diary. Did he contact you in the weeks before his death?"

Dalry cleared his throat. "As a matter-of-fact he did. I haven't told the police about it before now. Well, nobody had asked me, and I wasn't sure it was important."

"What did Mr Zhu want to know?"

"At first, he was telling me about a big party he had planned for Charmian next year. I told him it was a wonderful idea, but of course I would not be able to travel so far to attend. I'm nearly ninety, you know."

"Yes, I can imagine it would be difficult."

"Then we got chatting about Charmian's childhood here in Perth and Kinross. He was a most charming man to talk to. I was able to describe Charmian's Confirmation Mass, which took place when she was thirteen years old. I'd baptised her too, of course."

"You must have known the Wilson family very well."

"They were active members of my congregation. Anita helped with the flowers in the chapel on special occasions. It was a loss to the community when they moved away."

"Was Deming interested in anything else?"

"He was very curious about his wife's teenage years. It was awkward really, as Charmian became a difficult child for Anita and Colin during that period, which must have been around the mid-eighties. I wasn't sure how much Deming already knew."

"About the baby you mean?" Alice asked bluntly.

"Yes, as it happens. It wasn't a great secret. As Catholics, there was never a question of Charmian not having the child. I believe the infant was well looked after and adopted into a good household. I was involved with the family a great deal during that time. We insisted the child was baptised immediately after his birth. I didn't tell Deming all this, I wasn't sure if Charmian had shared this part of her history with him. It wasn't my place to break the news."

"Charmian went on to take her place at Oxford University. She must have calmed down her ways by then."

"The pregnancy matured her greatly. But it was a terrible strain on her parents. I sensed a wedge had formed between them. I tried to counsel the family as best I could but I fear the rift was never fully healed."

"Did you know who the father of the child was?"

Dalry sighed. "Charmian never told us. If she'd let me know during confession I wouldn't be able to divulge the name to you anyway, but the truth is she never did."

"Was there a boyfriend on the scene who it could have been?"

"Charmian had been staying out late in town and her parents suspected she'd skipped school on several occasions. The girl was very bright, but her parents brought her up strictly. As soon as she hit fifteen, the Wilsons had a rebellion on their hands."

"So, it could have been anyone in the town?"

"Yes, there were plenty of young people about in those days. They used to take the buses into Blair Atholl and even down to Perth. I'm afraid it could have been anyone, really."

Alice absorbed this information. "Thank you for your cooperation, Mr Dalry. You've been very helpful."

"It's Father Dalry, Inspector, if you don't mind." There was a brief pause on the line before he continued, "When you were in Beijing, did you visit Charmian in prison?"

"Yes, I did."

"Do you know if she has access to a priest?"

"I'm not sure, Father. We didn't know she was a Catholic then. It didn't occur to us to ask."

"I'm too old to travel so far to be by her side when the time comes, but Charmian must be allowed to make a final confession and be given the last rites by an ordained priest."

"Oh, okay. I'll see what I can do."

Dalry's voice became emphatic. "You must promise me, Inspector Mann. It is absolutely imperative."

"Yes, Father Dalry. If it's that important, I promise."

Chapter 27

The only establishments referred to as 'The Limes' in the Glasgow area tended to be doctors' surgeries. Andy couldn't understand what this might have to do with a lunch venue for Karla, Len and her parents.

He decided there could have been a pub or restaurant by that name operating in the spring of 1989 that no longer existed. There had been two major economic recessions since then. Plenty of businesses must have disappeared off the radar.

Sharon Moffatt approached Andy's desk. "I called Natalie Flynn, I hope you don't mind."

He shrugged his shoulders. "Not at all, the two of you built a rapport. Did she have anything to add?"

"I asked her about that holiday they took to France. Now Alan's clammed up I thought it was worth a try."

"How old was Natalie when they took the trip?"

"She was only four years old. It was a long shot." Sharon rested her ample figure on a swivel chair. "But according to Natalie, it's the only time they ever holidayed abroad during her childhood. The trip had stuck in her memory."

"Does she know where they stayed?"

"She remembers it was Normandy. Like Janet said, they stayed on a camp site. Natalie recalls making friends with the kids in the tent beside there's."

"Sounds like your average family holiday. What the hell could've been so significant about it?"

"What was significant is that they met another man there."

Andy sat bolt upright in his chair. "Dalgleish?"

"She'd no way of knowing that. Natalie just says she recalls him arriving at the campsite one day and parking his van behind their car alongside the tent. He sat on one of those low-slung camping chairs beside her father and they talked for hours. She remembered so clearly because they couldn't go to the beach that day due to the visit."

"Then Flynn and Dalgleish were definitely up to something."

"There's another thing."

"Oh, aye."

"The man didn't arrive on his own. There was a woman with him."

"*Karla?* I was beginning to think she didn't actually exist. Why wasn't she on the ferry?"

"I've no idea. But I pushed Natalie a bit about what this woman looked like. The description was pretty hazy; tall and slim, with dark hair and lots of makeup was all I got."

"That's not bad as a description. The only question is how reliable it is. We're talking about events from nearly thirty years ago and the recollections of a four year old."

"Yes, but we've finally got a sighting of this woman. That's got to be worth something."

*

James Irving thought his friend looked well. The weather was bright enough to risk sliding open the patio door to the flat's small, courtyard garden. Dani said she'd try to make it back for lunch, but there was no sign of her yet. He offered Howell a drink.

"I'll have a coffee, please. The car's outside."

"Sure, I'll prepare a pot. If Dani does make it home, she'll have to go back to the station again later. Best not to make it a boozy one!"

Howell smiled indulgently. "I don't really drink any longer, to be honest. Just the odd dram to help me sleep."

James busied himself finding the coffee beans, feeling suddenly awkward. "I've just rustled up some pasta puttanesca. Hope you don't mind something simple."

"A homecooked meal is always welcome when you spend a lot of time on the road."

"Are you due to tour again this year?"

Howell nodded. "I've another solo tour starting in September. The dates are booked already. But it's Europe this time. No long hauls."

James set the pot down on the table between them. "Did you make an appointment with Professor Morgan?" He asked tentatively.

Howell nodded. "Aye, I've met with him a couple of times now, at his flat in Kelvingrove."

"Has it been, err, helpful?"

Howell could see how much James was struggling. In all the years they'd known one another, they rarely had a heart-to-heart. Except perhaps when Dolly had died. "Yes, it has. I've spoken with therapists before but I found Professor Morgan to be more *interactive*."

"He's extremely knowledgeable. Rhodri has treated some very high profile patients."

"Criminals, you mean?"

"No, not all of them," James swiftly responded.

Howell laughed. "Don't worry, I was only pulling your leg. The professor told me lots of things about FAS. I'm not even sure that's what Dolly was suffering from now. The professor explained how many other conditions it was more likely to be."

James was pleased that Rhodri had put his friend's mind at ease. He hadn't deserved to suffer all these years. His body tensed as he heard the front door open.

Dani called down the corridor, "Hi! Am I too late for the food?"

James jumped out of his chair to greet her. "Not at all, I've not even dished up yet."

Dani shrugged off her jacket and sat down. "Great, I'm starving."

Howell grinned. "Thanks for making the time to come. James tells me you're on a big case."

"Yes, but my two sergeants are in charge. Right now, I'm covering for my DCS, who's off sick."

Howell furrowed his brow.

"The Detective Chief Superintendent. My boss."

"Ah, I see. He'd better watch out he's still got a job left when he gets back." Howell winked.

Dani chuckled, pleased to see the man appearing in such good spirits.

James placed a hand on her shoulder. "How is the case going?"

She tilted her head back. "Actually, we may have made some decent progress. We've nailed another member of the gang. He's gone quiet, but with a bit more pressure, he'll talk."

"Sounds ominous," Howell added.

"Not of the physical kind, I can assure you. Two of this man's associates have been murdered and another one is in Barlinnie. If he doesn't want to share their fate, he'll have to cooperate, sooner or later."

"Now," James said decisively, placing the pasta bowl in the centre of the table. "Let's forget about work and concentrate on eating."

"Sounds like a good plan," Dani replied with considerable feeling.

Chapter 28

Andy was back at the headquarters of the 5th Battalion of the Royal Regiment of Scotland. But it wasn't Captain Sutherland he was here to see. The DS had been granted a meeting with a Major Donald Marks. A sign he was being taken more seriously.

Marks sat behind a large oak desk. Another man, not in uniform, was positioned in the far corner.

"One of the Regiment's legal advisors," Marks explained, when Andy glanced in this man's direction. "We've been advised to record all our interactions with the police regarding the deaths of Corporal Addison and Private Garfield."

Andy took a seat. "Fair enough."

"Now, how may we help?"

"It has become evident that Addison, Garfield and Dalgleish sowed the seeds of their criminal partnership whilst serving with your regiment at the Girdwood Barracks in Belfast."

Marks interrupted. "They weren't actually involved in criminal activities during that time, I'm led to believe by the DCC."

"No, that's correct. But Dalgleish has been very candid. He says this was where the men discovered a shared interest in hardcore, exploitative pornography."

Marks's expression clouded with sadness. "You are too young to recall, DS Calder. For a British soldier garrisoned in Belfast during those years it was extremely tough. Our men were being murdered on a regular basis by Republican paramilitaries and our barracks frequently bombed. There was a long period of time when every British soldier dreaded turning the ignition key in their own cars. This was on Irish and British soil."

Andy nodded, contrary to Marks's assumption, he did recall the car bombs and the murders of loyalists. He knew it had gone on for much of the 80s and was only really halted by the peace agreements forged in the mid-90s.

"If those men took solace in pornographic magazines it would not have been unusual," the Major continued. "If we censored such activities we would be investigating half of the armed forces. It is not our job to police men's thoughts and desires, DS Calder."

Andy was quiet for a moment. He found himself in agreement with the man. "Yes, but it's clear that the barracks were Addison's recruiting ground. When I was here previously, I was furnished with a list of men who served alongside Dalgleish. What Captain Sutherland failed to give me, were the names of the men in the Catering Corps. It turns out one of those men was also part of this criminal gang."

Marks sighed. "This was an unfortunate oversight. Sutherland admits he hadn't taken your enquiry very seriously. I shall ensure that all of our records from Girdwood during that decade will be made available to your investigation."

Andy was taken aback. He'd expected more resistance. "Great. Your secretary can send them over to the incident room. We'll need the names of every Tom, Dick and Harry who was associated with the place – cooks, cleaners, decorators and gardeners, the whole nine yards." He suddenly realised the old-fashioned expression he'd used and added, "And women, too. We don't just want the names of the men who worked and served at

Girdwood. We want to know about the females as well."

Marks seemed unperturbed by the request. "Certainly. We'll get onto that straight away."

*

Angus Dunn was south Glasgow's version of a celebrity chef. His restaurant, The Pear Tree, had been open on Nelson Street for a couple of years. Business was booming. Dunn appeared as a guest on a popular television food programme and now his menu of locally sourced, seasonal dishes was in high demand.

Like many in his profession, the route to success hadn't been smooth. Dunn had hit the big time just when he should have been considering slowing down the pace a little, or even retiring. Angus had gone straight into catering from school and worked hard to learn his trade before opening his first restaurant in the late eighties.

His timing had been terrible. He bought the premises, down on the east coast, just before a major recession struck in the early nineties. No one was eating out any longer and the value of the building plummeted. Dunn went bust within three years. He was forced to turn to other avenues of business to make ends meet in the meantime.

Finally, he'd scraped together enough cash to put the deposit down on a restaurant that came up for sale on the Southside. He was lucky that a producer stumbled upon The Pear tree and loved his meal there. He insisted on meeting Angus afterwards and this conversation led to his gig on TV. The rest was history.

On this particular Friday night, the restaurant was full. Angus was working in the kitchen alongside his team. The customers loved it when he made an appearance at their table at some point in the evening. It was a big part of why they put their names on the waiting list and paid over the odds for the food. Angus had become a brand.

Service was intense. Angus could feel the heat of the top plates making the sweat stream from his brow. He reached for the towel that was tied around his waist, over his chef whites, and mopped the liquid from his face as it fell.

Angus glanced at his watch, it was nearly eleven, when the relentless grind began to slow-up a fraction. He felt immense relief, then a spasm of disappointment as he imagined doing the exact same thing the next night. Perhaps it was time for him to give up the grunt work. He certainly didn't enjoy it anymore.

His sous chef, a young lad from Paisley with an incredible future ahead of him placed his hand on Dunn's shoulder. "Why don't you take a break, boss? I've got the next set of orders covered."

Dunn nodded. "Aye, I might just do that."

The chef pushed through a side door and walked down the alleyway to the courtyard at the rear of the kitchens. He pulled a packet of Benson's out of his top pocket and lit up.

Dunn had considered converting the yard into an outdoor seating area. An alleyway ran along behind the far fence and it wasn't badly overlooked. But he'd been too busy the last few months to supervise the work. As it was, the yard had become a dumping ground for delivery crates and rubbish bags.

Over in the far corner, where the light from the kitchen window didn't reach, there was a shuffling noise behind one of the large, council bins.

Dunn shuddered, it was most likely rats. Another good reason to get the area overhauled. All the shit lying about was attracting vermin. Before long, they'd be making their way onto the premises. Dunn flicked his butt to the floor and ground it into the paving slabs. When they had it refurbed, he'd be sure to clear up his crap. Until then, it didn't make any odds if he added to the growing piles of litter.

The noise came again. It was louder now and sounded like it was being made by something bigger than a rat. A fox maybe.

Dunn stepped forward, peering into the gloom, "away with you," he called out, making shooing gestures with his arms.

His hand hit an object. It was too high to be one of the bins and too soft to be the fence. The object suddenly moved, a lunging motion that put Dunn off balance and sent him crashing to the concrete.

The chef automatically put his arms up in defence, but it was futile. A long blade was repeatedly stabbed into his body as he lay on the ground. The attack was so ferocious he barely had time to utter a protest and when it came, the words were simply a faint gurgling croak that wouldn't even have roused the rodents cowering in the dark.

Chapter 29

Alice had set off early and arrived in Pitlochry around midday. After a lengthy discussion with Fergus on Skype the previous evening, they both decided that it was worth doing some more digging into Charmian's teenage years there. Deming had clearly been very interested in this part of her life.

The house the Wilsons' had lived in during the 70s and 80s was on a leafy road near the distillery. Alice assessed it as a typical upper middle class residence; Victorian, double-fronted and with a sweeping pebble driveway. The Inspector had already checked who lived there now. The couple had only bought the property five years before. There was no point in interviewing them about the Wilson family, who'd been gone from the area at least ten years by then.

What Alice was relying on, was the list in Deming's notebook. A couple of the names had Pitlochry phone numbers. She'd retrieved their addresses from the police database.

Mandy Spicer lived in a semi-detached house off Larchwood Road. Alice parked her car outside on the quiet street. A middle-aged woman answered the door after a short delay.

Alice produced her warrant card. "Ms Spicer, my name is Inspector Alice Mann. I'd like to have a word with you, if I may?"

The woman took a step backwards, looking surprised. "Of course, come in. I was just outside in the garden, making the most of the good weather."

Alice nodded blandly, following Mandy into a bright kitchen.

"What's this about?" She asked tentatively. "You've got me quite worried."

"Please don't be. I'm in the area asking questions about Charmian Wilson, a lady who lived in Pitlochry as a child and adolescent. Your name cropped up in our enquiries. Did you know her?"

Mandy rested her weight on a bar stool. "Goodness, I've not heard that name in years. Yes, Charmian and I were very good pals at school. But we fell out of touch when she moved abroad."

"Did you know that Charmian has been convicted of a crime out in China. She is currently in prison."

A hand shot to the woman's thin, painted lips. "I didn't know that! What is she supposed to have done?"

Alice cleared her throat, wary of giving this poor woman too much to deal with at once. "She was accused of killing her husband, the businessman Deming Zhu. But her appeal team are working hard to get the conviction overturned."

"My Lord! How can they think that? Is there anything I can do to help! Why hasn't it been on the news?"

"The case has been reported in certain parts of the press, but Charmian is a Chinese citizen now and was living under Chinese law."

"I suppose you just don't imagine such a thing happening when you move abroad. Not that I'd fancy it much myself."

Alice leant forward. "Could you tell me as much as possible about Charmian when she lived here in Pitlochry. We believe that this knowledge may assist us."

Mandy scrunched up her face in concentration. "Charmian was very pretty and quite a determined person. Her parents were strict Catholics and they didn't allow Char to do much. Certainly not to wear make-up or short skirts. I suppose that's why she rebelled when we went up to the High School."

"Which school was that?"

"St Mary's in Blair Atholl. It was all-girls and we had to get on the bus together. This was the first taste of freedom either of us had experienced."

"The Wilsons' priest said they thought Charmian was skipping school."

Mandy grimaced. "Yes, she did. There were times when we had quiet study in the library. I used to cover for her when she slipped out."

"What was Charmian doing?"

Mandy looked embarrassed. "She had a boyfriend at the Catholic boys' school at the other end of town. I never had any boys interested in me at that age, so there was no problem with me holding the fort." She looked disgruntled.

"Do you recall this boy's name?"

"Och, it was a long time ago. He came from a big family, I remember that. They lived in a terraced house in Blair Atholl. Although they were a devout family, the weans ran pretty wild about the streets."

Alice softened her tone. "It's really important you try to recall, Mandy. This boy may have been the one who got Charmian pregnant."

The shock in the woman's face was obvious. "*Pregnant*? What are you talking about?"

"When Charmian was seventeen, she gave birth to a baby boy. He was adopted before she took her place at Oxford."

Mandy shook her head in disbelief. "Sweet Jesus, I never knew. Charmian's behaviour was getting worse. All of a sudden, her parents took her out of St Mary's. I tried to call on her at the house but they turned me away. It was only when Char was at

Oxford that she sent me a letter and we corresponded for a while. I had no idea there'd been a bairn."

Alice was inclined to believe her. "So, please try to think very carefully about this boy Charmian was involved with."

Mandy clasped her hands together. "He was a handsome lad, with thick, dark curly hair."

Alice immediately thought about Fergus.

"He was a wee bit older than Char, but not much. The family weren't long over from Ireland, I think. Wait a minute." Mandy got up and moved across to a bookcase. She took down a large, glossy hardback which seemed to be an illustrated local history book. "His Dad ran a grocery store on the main street. The name was above the door. I'm sure there's a picture of it in here." Mandy flicked through the pages.

Alice stood beside her, peering over her shoulder.

"There," Mandy said with satisfaction.

The photograph showed a bustling high street. It was taken in the early nineties. The grocery store was in the centre of the shot.

"Maguire's," Alice said quietly.

"I'm amazed I couldn't recall it. But there you are. The family were the Maguires of Blair Atholl."

Chapter 30

Dani stepped into the tent the SOCOs had erected. There wasn't a great deal of space in the restaurant's back yard. It appeared to have been used for general refuse.

The most striking thing about the murder scene were the blood stains on the man's white uniform. The contrast was quite dramatic in the cold light of early dawn. The pathologist was kneeling down beside the body. He turned to acknowledge the DCI's presence.

"Morning, Ma'am."

"What can you tell me?"

"Death occurred between 10pm last night and 2am this morning."

"His sous chef discovered him. Dunn came out for a cigarette at 11.05pm. He wasn't back within 20 minutes so his colleague went searching. We've got a nice narrow window for the murder to have occurred."

"Excellent. That makes my job easier. The cause of death looks straightforward – multiple stab wounds to the abdomen. But I can be more specific after the *PM*."

"Thanks. Keep me posted." Dani twisted round as Andy emerged along the side passage.

"We've finished interviewing the staff, Ma'am. We let the remaining customers go a few hours back." Andy averted his gaze from the body. "According to the kitchen staff, nobody followed Dunn out of the side door. I think we've got to assume the perp approached along the rear passageway and over the fence."

"Yes, that's the most plausible explanation."

Andy tipped his head to the side. "The sous chef claims his boss came out the back for a fag at the end of each night's service."

"A bit of a habit, then?"

"Which means the killer was either watching the back of the place to suss out his routines, or they were getting information from someone inside."

"We need to bear both theories in mind. The sous chef found the body. How shaken up was he?"

"The poor lad's vomited up his own body weight since last night. We had to get the doc to take a look at him. I don't imagine he could've had the stomach for it." Andy paused as his mobile phone started to buzz. "Sorry, Ma'am, it's DS Moffett."

"Take it, it could be important."

Andy nodded and put the phone to his ear. He listened intently for a few minutes. His eyes grew wider the more he heard. "Thanks Sharon, great work. I'll see you back at the station in 20 minutes."

"What is it?" Dani was intrigued by his reaction.

"I left Sharon going through the list I was emailed from the 5th Regiment last night. I requested the names of all the people who worked at the Girdwood Barracks between '78 and '90. One name leapt out at her."

Dani raised her eyebrows expectantly.

Andy dipped his head towards the body. "A young Angus Dunn was a member of the Army Catering Corps stationed at Girdwood. He worked alongside Alan Flynn as one of the kitchen hands."

"Right then. It seems we've got ourselves a serial offender."

*

Dani stood in front of the evidence board in the de-briefing suite. She stepped towards the flip chart and began listing names:

Len Dalgleish
Kenneth Garfield
Robert Addison
Alan Flynn
Angus Dunn

The DCI stood back. "Three of these men have been murdered. We have to assume that Len is only alive because he's still in prison."

"Do we think Alan Flynn needs protection, Ma'am?" Andy put in.

Dani sighed. "Much as I'm reluctant to waste public money on the scumbag, I suspect you're right. I'll get a couple of uniforms over to the Crosshouse Estate to stand outside their flat." She turned back to the chart. "These men all met at the Girdwood Barracks in Belfast, during the height of 'The Troubles'; between 1978 and the mid to late 80s. Len, Kenneth and Robbie were soldiers and Alan and Angus were cooks."

Sharon had been staring hard at the flip-chart, her eyes blurring as the names swam around in her vision, crossing over one another and continually altering their position. She suddenly leapt to her feet. "Karla!" She exclaimed.

Dani was taken aback. "Yes, we also picked up on a reference to a woman called Karla in Dalgleish's personal effects. But we've yet to make a conclusive identification of this person."

"No, Ma'am," Sharon continued excitedly. "I mean it's an anagram, or an acronym possibly."

Andy was lost already.

Sharon strode across to the chart and picked up a marker pen. "Look, if you take the first letter of each man's name and put them in a different order."

The DS wrote out another list, beside her boss's:

Kenneth Garfield
Alan Flynn
Robbie Addison
Len Dalgleish
Angus Dunn

Andy screwed up his face. "The first letters of their names spell KARLA. What the hell does it mean?"

Dani was silent for a few minutes, her mind ticking over. "Can we see those love letters again, Andy?"

Calder went back to his workstation and fished the copies he'd made out of their file.

Dani scanned through the contents. "These letters appear to be correspondence between a pair of lovers. But what if, like DS Moffett suggests, KARLA was an acronym for the men's illegal outfit."

Andy knew the wording of the correspondence better than anyone else in the room. "If you ignore the lovey-dovey stuff, the main thrust of those letters related to two plans to meet up. The first was at a place called 'The Limes', here in the Glasgow area and the second was the holiday in France."

"Those letters were sent in the mid to late eighties," Sharon added. "This was a period of time with no text messages or emails. No World Wide Web. If these men wanted to send instructions to each other that others couldn't intercept or properly understand, they'd use coded letters."

"And the code for the gang was Karla," Dani stated flatly.

Andy shook his head in confusion. "Was there ever a woman involved at all? What about the lassie Natalie Flynn saw at the campsite in Normandy?"

"She could simply have been a woman Len picked up during his travels."

"Or one of the girls they were trafficking back to Scotland to make pornos for them," Dan Clifton suggested.

"But more importantly," Dani stated with emphasis. "Who is it that's killing them off? Picking them out and butchering them, one by one?"

"I reckon they got themselves wrapped up with some eastern European mafia types. They provided the girls for a fee. Now the Scottish gang has been busted, one of the mafia bosses is kicking over the traces." Andy's expression was resolute.

Dani frowned, whilst looking again at the crime scene photos. "I just don't get the feeling these murders are professional hits. Wouldn't a people trafficking gang have access to guns? they're easy enough to get hold of on the continent."

"But not so easy to smuggle into this country these days, Ma'am," Sharon inserted. "The anti-terrorism laws have really toughened up border procedures."

Dani nodded. "Okay, we keep the international crime angle open. Andy can share the details of the murders with Interpol. In the meantime, we work the Dunn killing like we would any other on our patch. We take statements from neighbours, scour the CCTV on Nelson Street and put out an appeal for witnesses." She ran a hand through her shoulder-length hair. "And it's time to stop chasing this Karla character. I think we can agree she doesn't exist. She's a phantom created by some very bad men to throw us off the scent, so let's not allow it to."

Mutters of agreement rippled around the room. But Sharon Moffett remained silent. Despite cracking the acronym, the image of Karla was still inside her head. Tall, pretty, with wavy dark hair.

Just like the description Natalie had given her. It was an image that would prove difficult for the detective to shift.

Chapter 31

Maguire's grocery store no longer stood in the centre of Blair Atholl High Street. In its place was a gift shop selling tourist trinkets and postcards of the castle.

According to the database, there were no more Maguires living in the area. At some point, the entire family had moved away. Without the name of the boy Charmian had been meeting up with all those years ago, it was going to prove tricky to track him down.

St Mary's School was still going strong. Alice stood outside the wrought iron gates which framed a Victorian building of grey stone. There was no point in asking questions there, the staff teaching back in the eighties would all be retired now.

The detective had one more name to check out from Deming's list. The address was in Killiecrankie, roughly half way back to Pitlochry on the main road.

The place she was looking for turned out to be a flat within a larger house. Alice had waited until after 7pm in the hope the owner would be at home.

After a few seconds, a woman in her early sixties, with a mass of grey girls and a long, smock-like woollen dress opened up.

Alice showed her ID. "Karen Wiley? My name is Inspector Mann. May I come inside?"

The woman frowned, revealing deep lines across her forehead. Her posture became defiant. "For what reason?"

This was the first time Alice had experienced hostility since arriving in Perthshire. "I'm assisting in the appeal case against the murder conviction of

Charmian Zhu, neé Wilson. I believe this woman is your niece? Anita Wilson is your older sister?"

The woman nodded reluctantly. "That's correct. What do you mean an *appeal*? Anita told me the situation was hopeless. She and Colin have written her off."

"Well, there are others who have not. A very dedicated team of Edinburgh lawyers are still hoping to gain a stay of execution. Perhaps reduce the sentence to life imprisonment."

Karen glanced about her at the empty corridor. "It's not a good idea to talk about this here. You'll have to come inside."

The flat was lacking in natural light. Karen Wiley hadn't helped this situation by filling the place with African style carvings of dark wood and thick, oriental looking tapestries hanging from the walls and draped across the furniture.

"Have a seat," she offered begrudgingly.

Alice sat down. "I got your name and address from a notebook belonging to Charmian's husband. Did Deming Zhu call you in the weeks before his death?"

Karen looked sceptical. "Will this really help Charmian's case?"

"I don't know. But to be honest, we don't have much time left. Anything I can discover about the circumstances of the couple has got to be better than nothing."

Karen nodded in solemn agreement. "Aye, Deming called me in February some time. He was talking about a big shin-dig for Char over in Beijing. I've no idea why he rang me about it. I haven't got two ha'pennies to rub together. I'm not sure my niece would have wanted me in her shiny new life anyways."

"Why do you say that?"

"We were close when Char was little. Anita and Colin were so authoritarian. The poor wee thing had no freedom whatsoever. She was in Mass most of Sunday and helping her mum with the garden on a Saturday. I used to take her out and treat her every now and again. Which wasn't hard, as Char never did anything fun."

"Did your niece confide in you?"

Karen shrugged. "When she was a girl, yes. But Char rebelled a bit as a teenager, then she became secretive." The woman narrowed her eyes suspiciously. "You know about the bairn, I suppose?"

Alice nodded. "Yes, I do."

"Well, that was a catastrophe for Char. She had to tell her parents and that meant surrendering all her power to them. Anita, Colin and the priest organised the confinement and adoption. After that I barely saw my niece. She went off to study down south. I imagine Char worked as hard as she could to get away from her parents. She rejected her old life."

"Do you know who the father of the baby was? I have a feeling it might be important. I think Deming was trying to find this information out before he died." Alice decided to place her cards on the table.

Karen looked pensive. "I thought he was asking a lot of questions. It seemed odd after so many years of showing no interest. I would never have told him about the bairn, though. Not without checking with Char first."

"How much do you know?"

"I was living out near the barracks in those days."

Alice furrowed her brow in puzzlement.

"The army barracks near the Girnaig forest. They used to do their exercises in there. I rented a cottage on the edge of the nearby village. I wanted to be close to Ian."

"Ian?"

"My boyfriend. He was a soldier at the barracks. We met at one of the pubs in Pitlochry. We were engaged to be married back then."

Alice glanced about the dingy flat. There was no evidence of another occupant. "What happened?"

"He was killed," she replied abruptly. "But back in the early-eighties we were very happy. Char used to take the bus to see us. I knew she was skipping school but I never told Anita. I don't understand why she packed the poor girl off to be taught by all those miserable nuns. It's so arcane."

"Charmian's school friend told me it was a boy in Blair Atholl that she was seeing. A lad from a big Irish family there."

Karen looked surprised. "One of the Maguire boys?"

"Yes, that's right." Alice waited expectantly.

The woman shook her head vigorously. "No, she would never have been involved with them. Char had enough Catholicism shoved down her throat as a child, she'd hardly have hooked up with one of *them*."

Alice sensed she'd hit on a raw nerve. "Who did you think the father was, then?"

Karen got to her feet, upsetting a small Indian table as she did so, knocking it to the floor and its contents of magazines. "We never knew. I *told* you. Char was full of secrets back then. But it wasn't like you're suggesting. Someone's lying to you, making trouble. I'd like you to leave."

Alice wasn't quite sure what she'd said to offend the woman, but she allowed herself to be jostled to the front door. "I'm sorry, I didn't mean to upset you."

Karen shot her a pained look as she shoved the

young detective over the threshold and swung the door firmly shut.

Alice was left in the empty corridor feeling shell-shocked, but convinced she'd stumbled upon something big.

Chapter 32

"Nelson Street isn't the kind of place where folk notice strangers on the pavement from behind their chintzy net curtains," Andy grumbled.

"It's all eateries, with maybe the odd flat up above," Dan Clifton agreed. "On Friday night, each of the restaurants was busy with customers. The staff and clientele weren't interested in what was going on outside."

"I suppose our perp was counting on that." Sharon placed three coffee cups in the centre of the table. "Help yourselves," she added, pulling a packet of chocolate digestives out of a drawer and placing it down too.

"Ta," Dan said eagerly, tearing open the top of the packet and grabbing a mug.

Andy found Sharon a breath of fresh air compared to the up-tight and perpetually health conscious Alice Mann. "Gaskill's still sifting through the CCTV. That passage behind the restaurant comes out by the car park near Tradeston Street. Unfortunately, there are no cameras in there. It's run by the council and they've not enough money for decent security."

"Do we think the killer had a get-away vehicle parked in there?" Sharon rested on the edge of the desk and sipped her coffee.

"Aye, almost certainly. Dunn's restaurant was a sitting target, a criminal's wet dream."

"Any forensics left on the body?" Dan asked.

"Naw, the blood was Dunn's. The pathologist

reckons he fell backwards before the onslaught. There wasn't an opportunity for him to get a blow landed on his attacker. There were defence wounds all over the hands and lower arms of the victim."

"This job was well planned. The perp would've been gloved up. I expect he's disposed of the weapon and clothing by now." Sharon sighed.

"Did the restaurant have its own CCTV?" Dan enquired, a note of desperation in his voice.

"No. Apparently, they bank up most evenings and don't keep money on the premises."

"The back yard was just full of rubbish. I don't suppose they thought surveillance was necessary."

"Angus Dunn clearly wasn't expecting to be targeted. What do we know about his life after he left the Catering Corps?"

Sharon flipped open her notebook. "He worked in various kitchens in the late eighties, finally becoming a head chef after two years. He set up his own restaurant in Largs in '88. But it must have closed down because he was working in other people's kitchens again until opening the restaurant on Nelson Street in 2014. The place has been doing really well, according to the manager."

"What's the name of the restaurant, again?" Andy asked abruptly.

"The Pear Tree."

He sat up straighter in his seat. "Do we know what the original restaurant was called – the one he opened on the east coast in '88?"

Sharon looked embarrassed. "I don't know. I got all that info from a biography the Herald ran last year, after Dunn appeared on *Saturday Morning Cooks*."

"If it closed down, might there be bankruptcy records?" Dan suggested. "My uncle lost his business in the recession and had to publish all his assets at Companies House. It's something to do with satisfying the creditors."

"As you seem to know so much about it, Dan, can you check that out for me? And if that restaurant turns out to have been called 'The Limes', I'll buy you both a very large drink."

*

Andy was reclining on the sofa in his sitting room with his feet up on the coffee table. Amy was snuggled up next to him, scribbling intently in a Disney Frozen colouring book.

The phone in his pocket started to buzz. He grumbled bitterly under his breath, trying his best not to swear. "Calder," he barked.

"Andy? It's Alice Mann. Sorry to bother you in the evening."

He sat bolt upright, causing Amy to complain as one of her pens rolled down the gap between the cushions. *"Alice,* how're you doing? Not ringing from the Great Wall of China I hope."

Alice chuckled. "Not quite, more like The Golden Dragon on Renfrew Street."

"You're back then?"

"Yes, I've been home a few days. How's the investigation going?" She felt immediately guilty asking.

"The body count is rising, but the victims are all scumbags, so I'm not losing any sleep over it."

"I really am sorry I left you in the lurch over the Dalgleish investigation."

"You couldn't have known it was going to escalate in the way it did. Besides, DS Moffett's been a good addition to the team. I hope Bevan keeps her on afterwards."

"Oh," Alice paused. "I'm glad it's worked out."

"But there's no need to feel pushed out. You'll like her too. We still need a DI."

"Sure, I'm looking forward to working with her." Alice cleared her throat. "The reason I called, was to get some advice. I'm still investigating for the Charmian Zhu appeal and its brought me back to her hometown in Perthshire."

"Oh aye."

"I've made a few enquiries already in the area and several names have cropped up. I just needed to bounce my ideas off somebody – to ensure I'm not embarking on a flight of fancy."

Andy settled back into his seat, slipping his arm around Amy and hugging her tight, feeling strangely pleased that Alice had chosen to confide in him. "Go on then, tell me the full story," he said.

Chapter 33

DC Dan Clifton approached his boss tentatively. Andy raised his head from his computer screen. "What have you got for me?"

Dan slipped a piece of paper under Andy's nose. "The place was called 'The Lime Tree'. Is that close enough to earn me a pint?"

"Depends what else you've discovered."

"The restaurant opened on the 25th April 1989 on the esplanade in Largs. Within a matter of months, the country had plummeted headlong into the worst recession since the war. The place closed its doors in December '93. Dunn filed for bankruptcy the same month. I've got lists of creditors and the details of the bank foreclosure on his start-up loan. But within four years, he'd paid off all his debt. We're talking about tens of thousands."

Andy rubbed his chin. "Even if he'd objected to Robbie's scheme to start the pornography business, Angus Dunn wouldn't have had much choice but to get involved after his restaurant went bust."

"Maybe he just got mixed up with Addison and the others to clear the debts. Dunn may have opted out when his catering business finally became successful?"

"Even if that's the case, someone out there thought he was involved enough to warrant silencing, along with all the others." Andy narrowed his eyes. "Do you think 'The Limes' could have been a nickname for Dunn's first restaurant? Was that where the men originally met to discuss their plans?"

Dan shrugged his shoulders. "It could be. They

certainly enjoyed being cryptic in their correspondence."

"That's true enough."

Sharon Moffett approached her colleagues, a smile on her face. "We've just had confirmation from the tech lab. The body recovered from The Firth of Lorn is definitely that of Robert Addison. The lab had managed to extract some DNA from the body. They compared it to a sample volunteered by Addison's niece. There was enough of a match for us to be certain."

"Well, that's something." Andy nodded encouragingly. "Good work."

"I'll pass that on. The techies were keen to tell me how tough it was to find DNA traces after the body had been so long in the water. The cold temperatures saved the day."

"But on a cause of death, they can't be so sure?"

Sharon shook her head despondently. "The body was bashed about beyond recognition by the propeller of the ferry. It's impossible to identify if the injuries were delivered *pre* - or *post-mortem*. Our working assumption must be that Addison was knocked unconscious or dead before being dumped into the sea. But we can't prove it."

"It could still be suicide," Dan offered weakly, expecting to receive the sharp end of Calder's tongue for delivering the bad news.

Instead, Andy sighed deeply. "Aye, it could. But with Dunn murdered *after* Addison was found swimming with the fishes, he's unlikely to be our perp. The problem is, we've no other suspect."

Sharon pursed her lips. "Then we need to find one. Let's go back to all the places and people who connect these five men. We ask questions, knock on doors and kick over every stone. This killer must have left some kind of trace, however small."

Andy got to his feet. "You're right Sharon. Let's stop feeling sorry for ourselves and start jogging a few memories out there.

*

Fergus Kelso sat on an uncomfortable plastic chair in the waiting room of the maximum security prison. He was fortunate to have been granted another visit with Charmian. Kelso could tell that his colleagues back in Edinburgh were losing hope of being able to file a successful appeal. He couldn't help but suspect David Acomb had spoken with his head of chambers and warned them off.

Finally, the guard standing by the door to the visiting rooms received a message on his walkie-talkie and beckoned for Fergus to follow him.

Charmian was sitting very still, head bowed low over the table as the lawyer entered. He noticed how her pale, thin wrists were red-raw under the metal handcuffs. The sight made him feel irrationally angry. He breathed the emotion back.

"Mrs Zhu, this may be our last meeting. I need to ask you some more important questions."

Charmian raised her gaze. Her expression was weary. "Is there really any point, Mr Kelso? I received a letter from your boss encouraging me to prepare for the worst."

"He shouldn't have sent that. Not yet. We are still investigating."

Charmian narrowed her eyes and looked at him appraisingly. "Who is *we*? You and the red-headed girl who was here before? Why are you still trying to save me? Everyone else has given up. Even my own parents." The words were spoken with curiosity, not self-pity.

Fergus leant forward. "You're a Scottish citizen, you don't deserve this. I don't believe you committed the crime."

Charmian's body slumped backwards against the hard chair. "My God, to finally meet an idealist, at this of all moments in my life!"

"Your husband was investigating you. He contacted your parents in France and made them provide him with lists of people from your childhood in Pitlochry. This was during the weeks before his death. Do you know why?"

Charmian's body jerked upright. "Why was Deming doing that?"

"We aren't sure. Perhaps because he'd found something out about your past. He wanted to investigate further."

Charmian's eyes darted from left to right. "What did he find out?" She looked terrified.

"We can't tell. But I'd be very surprised if he didn't discover you'd had a baby back then. It wouldn't have been difficult."

Charmian allowed her head to fall into her hands. "He never said a word. Why didn't he ask *me* about it? Why go behind my back?"

"You never told your husband about the child you had adopted when you were seventeen?"

She glanced up, her eyes wild. "Why would I? It was a lifetime ago. I barely admitted it even to myself." Her expression suddenly changed, as recognition appeared to dawn on her. She shuffled forward and grasped Fergus's hands. "Did you speak with Jia?"

Fergus nodded, the feeling of his mother's skin against his own was oddly electric.

"Deming had been courting a new client, I remember now that his name was Schrager. He's an American. My husband said one night over dinner how convinced he was the businessman was having him closely vetted before signing over his investments." Charmian's grip tightened. "Perhaps Schrager investigated Deming *and* me. He may have found out about the baby and my early life in Scotland. Perhaps he felt duty bound to tell Deming what he'd discovered about my past. The two men had become friends. That may have been what spurred Deming on to find out more."

Fergus considered this possibility. "You may be right. It was during the time Schrager was becoming a client of Asia Trust Management when your husband began contacting people from your past."

"That must be it." She shook her head desperately. "What did he find out?"

Fergus held her gaze. "You tell me, Mrs Zhu. Because I believe whatever he did find out was what led to his murder and your incarceration. But if anyone can tell us what information that was, it's you."

"There's nothing to tell. My parents were extremely strict. I was an only child and they placed a heavy burden of expectation on me. When I hit teenage, I rebelled. But only by the pathetic standards of my wee highland town."

"You skipped school and met with a boy your parents wouldn't have approved of."

"Your pretty friend has obviously been doing her homework. Yes, that's basically how it was. I found a handsome rogue, a few years older than me and we fell in love. I adored him and his strong principles and would have done anything for him. Then, in the summer of '84, I discovered I was pregnant. My whole world fell apart. I was seventeen and had led an extremely sheltered life. I didn't know what to do."

"You told your parents?"

"My Mother." Charmian dropped her eyes to examine her dirty, bitten nails. "The worst mistake I ever made. They abhorred the idea of a termination. The baby was to be born and adopted into a good, religious family. Then, I would continue my education before spending the rest of my days making up for my terrible sins."

"If you'd had your way, the baby wouldn't have been born?" Fergus's voice sounded distant, even to himself.

Charmian sighed. "No, I'm not saying that. I was so brainwashed by the good Father Dalry that I don't think I would have got rid of it. Then there was the question of the father. That would have stopped me having an abortion."

"Why? Did he know about the baby?"

Charmian shook her head violently. "I never told him. There wasn't time. My parents had whisked me away into confinement by then. And once the baby was there and the adoption finalised, I was off to Oxford."

Fergus glanced frantically at his watch. "Do you believe that Deming discovered who the father was? Was this the information that got him killed?"

Charmian seemed totally confused. "I don't see how. Our relationship was a secret. I've no idea where he is now, or if he's even still alive. I've often thought he might be in prison. I just don't know."

One of the guards pulled Charmian away by the arm. Her hands slipped out of the young lawyer's grasp.

"But he *was* one of the Maguires?" Fergus threw the question at her as she was led from the room. "Which of the boys was he, Mrs Zhu?"

Charmian turned, the half-flickering of a smile playing on her parched lips. "Strangely, you remind me of him. He was an idealist too, in his own way."

She chuckled as she passed through the security door. "It must be the tiredness and hunger playing tricks."

Chapter 34

DI Alice Mann stood outside what was once the Moraig Barracks, just outside Aldclune. The council officer she spoke with that morning informed her the area was designated for a new housing estate and primary school.

Right now, the land was still populated with abandoned Nissan huts. A small, one-storey brick building with broken windows and pealed paintwork dominated the plot. There wasn't much left to indicate the military operation that had once thrived there.

After her conversation with Andy Calder, Alice went back to the notes of her interview with Karen Wiley. As Andy had patiently relayed the details of his own case, he'd described the oppressive atmosphere that pervaded the British army of the eighties and early nineties which triggered the descent into crime of a group of Glasgow ex-squadies. These men were now being picked off by a brutal killer; one by one.

During that era, the IRA had been particularly active. Most soldiers during the period would have spent time in Northern Ireland. But even back home in Scotland, the risks for servicemen were high. Andy had told her of his surprise at discovering the sheer number of bombings of UK barracks that took place, even into the early nineties.

This statement had piqued Alice's interest. Charmian's aunt had talked about living near the barracks when her niece fell pregnant. She'd talked of a partner called Ian, who was stationed there at the time.

The year Charmian Wilson became pregnant with Fergus was 1984. She gave birth in early '85, but by then she was well away from the Pitlochry area.

Alice picked her way along a stony path to a wire fence which encircled the site. The council official hadn't given her permission to enter. The area still needed to be thoroughly cleared and made safe before the developers could even be let in to demolish what was left. With re-designated MOD land, there was always a risk of live ammunition and shells turning up in the soil.

Right in the centre of the plot, the DI could make out a small crater in the earth. To the unsuspecting eye, it would appear to be a natural dip in the landscape. The developers would surely fill it in before they began to build. But Alice knew the cause of this strange geographic feature.

According to the newspaper reports she'd read in the online archives, a 15lb time bomb ripped through the accommodation building of the Moraig Barracks at 5.15am on Tuesday 7th February, 1984. The timing of the detonation designed to cause maximum casualties.

19 soldiers were killed in the blast, including 28 year-old Corporal Ian Corry, Karen Wiley's boyfriend. Within hours of the explosion, the provisional IRA claimed responsibility for the bombing. Alice discovered that a local man named Patrick Callan was arrested within days of the atrocity. A neighbour reported unusual comings and goings from his property in Blair Atholl in the weeks before the bomb was planted.

Local police found a basic bomb making facility in an upstairs bedroom. Traces of nitrobenzene were discovered on his clothes and a detonator found in Callan's possession. The authorities knew Callan wasn't acting alone, but the man wouldn't talk about his accomplices, or how he gained access to the barracks so easily. Patrick Callan was convicted of multiple murder and was sentenced to life imprisonment. He served 14 years of that sentence, but was released in 1998, under the terms of the Good Friday Agreement.

Alice hadn't been able to ascertain where Callan lived now. She assumed he'd returned to his hometown of Kilkeel, Northern Ireland. The DI thought about the young Charmian Wilson, who had fallen in love with a boy from an Irish family in Blair Atholl, at the same time as the IRA were planning a devastating attack on the area which required local knowledge and assistance on the ground. She wondered if the investigating officers knew about Charmian's connection to Ian Corry, through her maternal aunt. She imagined they didn't.

The DI walked slowly back to her car. She climbed into the driver's seat, preparing to head back towards Killiekrankie, for a confrontation she wasn't relishing.

*

Alice pressed the doorbell for the second time. She could make out movement inside. The door had a spyhole and the detective was certain that someone was standing directly on the other side, peering through it.

"Ms Wiley, we spoke the other day about your niece, Charmian. Some new evidence has come to light. I really need to talk to you."

The silence was charged with tension.

"Please open up. If you don't, I'll have to shout the information through this door. I'm not sure you'd like the neighbours to hear what I have to say." Alice deliberately raised her voice.

After a brief pause, Alice heard the deadlock being turned. The door opened a crack.

"Is this *really* necessary?" Karen's voice hissed through the narrow space between the door and the frame.

"Yes, it is." Alice shoved the door open, aware she'd knocked the woman backwards, and proceeded down the hallway to the dark living room.

Karen followed along behind, dropping down onto her cluttered sofa with resignation.

"When we last spoke, you didn't tell me about the bombing at the barracks, which occurred just weeks before Charmian told her parents she was pregnant." Alice remained standing.

Karen's lined face clouded with sadness. "Why would I? It was horrific, for the entire community. But it had nothing to do with Charmian."

Alice felt her words lacked conviction. "Tell me what happened."

"I was living in a cottage, on the outskirts of the woods surrounding the barracks. I wanted to be close to Ian. We weren't married yet, but we'd talked about it." Her hands clasped tightly in her lap. For the first time, Alice noticed the simple silver ring on the third finger of her left hand. "The explosion woke me up. I looked at the bedside clock. It was nearly twenty past five. I knew immediately what it was. It's hard to imagine now, but in those days every serviceman and his family had learnt to dread that moment."

"What did you do?"

"I was shaking uncontrollably. It was all I could manage to pull some clothes on over my nightie. I ran out the front of the cottage. There were others standing by their gates already. All of them looking upwards at the plume of smoke rising into the dawn sky beyond the trees."

"I'm very sorry for your loss."

"I knew he was dead. Folk will say its fanciful, but I felt a terrible emptiness straight away. The lads in dorm C took the brunt of the blast. That included Ian. He wouldn't have known anything about it." Karen glanced up and caught the detective's eye. "Believe me, that's a great comfort. There were others who were badly injured. A few died later in hospital."

"A man called Patrick Callan was convicted of the bombing."

"That's right. Callan had been working in one of the hotels in Pitlochry. He'd been over from Ireland for a year or so. The police said he'd had links to the IRA for over a decade. He made the bomb in his spare bedroom."

The banality of the words filled Alice with sadness. "The police didn't believe Callan had operated alone."

Karen shook her head. "Other men were seen entering Callan's property in the days before the bombing. It's the reason his neighbours called the police for heaven's sake!"

"But these men were never identified?"

"No, but we all had our suspicions."

"What do you mean?"

Karen's expression became steely. "We all knew that the Maguire boys were republican sympathisers. Ian understood to steer well clear of the pubs they frequented."

"But there was no evidence to suggest they were involved?"

Karen snorted. "A couple of weeks after the bombing, Frank Maguire took the whole family to Ireland for his mother's funeral. Only Frank and his wife came back."

"The boys remained in Ireland?"

Karen shrugged. "They may have gone to the USA. There was a great deal of Irish republican support over there in those days. But the implication is obvious. The Maguire boys fled the area after the barracks were bombed. The evidence was pretty damning."

"But circumstantial," Alice added.

Karen shook her mop of hair in frustration. "You had to have been there. Those lads were firebrands, full of anger for the authorities. We all knew they were responsible." The woman jerked to attention, as if a memory had just returned to her. "And the younger one, Aiden, he'd worked for a company that delivered to the barracks. The boy had sat in the van dozens of times, passing in and out of the place, helping to unload."

Alice thought this would have been enough to warrant an interview with the Maguire boys back then, but without any provable connection to Callan, or any forensic evidence linking them to the bomb, they couldn't have charged them. "What about the older brother?"

"Ciaran? He was the charmer. Smooth and good-looking. Who would've thought such a beautiful boy could have caused so much horror and pain."

Alice took a breath, perching on the arm of a chair. "When I was here before, I said that Charmian may have been involved with one of the Maguire sons."

Karen wrung her hands together. "I've thought of nothing else since."

"Do you think Charmian's schoolfriend could have been right?"

Karen arched her back and closed her eyes, as if in pain. "She was only a wee girl at heart, despite her attempts to rebel against her parents. Charmian came to my cottage off the bus. She'd sit in the front room and drink tea with me out of the pot. We chatted about school; all the teachers she hated and those she liked. Charmian always showed an interest in me – in *us*. She got on well with Ian, too. Forever asking him questions about his job and what it was like to live and work in the barracks. Charmian was a very bright, switched on girl."

Alice cleared her throat. "Charmian asked Ian about the barracks?" she said tentatively. "What sort of questions?"

Karen began fidgeting with the tassels of an oriental patchwork throw covering the battered upholstery of the old sofa. "She was interested in their routines – what time they got up, how the dormitories were set out, that kind of thing. I thought it was her natural curiosity. As a toddler, Charmian never stopped asking questions."

Alice had moved quietly across the room and placed a hand on the woman's shoulder. "And when was she making these inquiries, Karen?"

Her body had begun shaking with sobs. "It was before she knew she was pregnant," Karen spluttered. "In the weeks leading up to the February of 1984."

Chapter 35

Rusty was pulling hard on his lead, frustrated after many hours spent tied up in the garden.

Natalie Flynn's arm was aching with the effort it was taking to keep him at heal. She was relieved when the path ended at an open field where the dog could be let off the leash.

She stood and watched him bolt through the long grass, chasing first after the tennis ball he'd been tossed and then a leaf being blown about on the breeze. Natalie chuckled at his stupidity. Abruptly, the laughter froze on her lips.

The woman's thin body was suddenly enclosed in an iron grip, the breath being almost squeezed out of her by the two, thick arms strapped across her chest. She glanced desperately in the direction of the puppy, who was at least a quarter of a mile away, his nose buried in a rabbit hole.

A face pressed itself up to hers. A husky voice whispered chillingly in her ear. "Tell your Daddy that I'm coming for him. He can't hide in that flat forever. The police aren't going to care about a dirty scumbag like him. Security won't be too tight. When I eventually get your filthy Daddy alone, I'm going to make him perform for the camera – if you know what I mean. Right before I slit his stinking throat."

Rusty finally turned, to check in with his owner. The site of the stranger, silhouetted on the horizon, sent the dog into a frenzy of barking. He dashed back towards Natalie as the dark figure disappeared into the trees leaving the woman in a heap on the cold ground. Rusty ignored the retreating assailant, leaping onto the prone body of his mistress instead, covering her face with his wet, slobbering tongue.

*

Dani accompanied Andy to the hospital. There was some concern from the DCC's office that Flynn's parents might lodge a complaint.

Andy led the way to the woman's room. "I've spoken with the doctors, Ma'am. Natalie Flynn is absolutely fine. She's a wee bit shaken up, but no physical injuries beyond a few bruises to the ribs."

"And you had no reason to believe she was in danger?"

Andy shook his head. "This maniac is after Addison's gang. I don't think they'll harm the families. Natalie was targeted as a warning to her Da'. Because he can't be reached."

Dani sighed. "I suppose we should have predicted it."

Andy grunted. "We can't protect Alan Flynn's entire family, Ma'am. The DCC can't possibly expect that."

"No, and he'd never give us the funding to do it either. But it won't stop him raking me over the coals when there's a fuck up."

Andy was tutting loudly as he knocked on the door and pushed it open.

Natalie Flynn looked tiny lying in the centre of the white sheets. Her face was pale and troubled.

Dani moved across and took the seat by her bedside. "Natalie, my name is DCI Dani Bevan. I'm very sorry you had to go through that ordeal. It must have been terrifying."

Natalie levered herself up on her elbows. "Is Rusty okay?"

Dani nodded, a little impatiently. "Yes, he's at the kennels of a local station. You'll be able to pick him up after you're discharged."

"Good." She fell backwards onto the pillows.

"Miss Flynn, did you get a look at the person who attacked you?"

She shook her head of limp hair. "No, I was grabbed from behind. I wasn't really attacked. I was being given a message."

"And what was the message?" Andy flipped open his notebook.

"That my Dad was a dead man. He was going to get his throat cut." She looked like she might be sick.

"We'll need a statement with the exact wording," Dani said gently.

"Your father is under police protection," Andy added more forcefully. "Nobody's going to get to him."

Natalie's eyes flashed with anger. "For how long? You don't really care about him – you think he's a scumbag who deserves everything he gets. That's why they'll reach him in the end!"

Dani narrowed her eyes. "Is that what the man who accosted you said? That we didn't really care about protecting your father?"

"Yes," Natalie retorted. "And it's true. He won't be safe forever."

Dani didn't quite know how to respond to this. Her father would never be safe if they didn't nail the killer. "Then you need to tell us everything you can about this person – his smell; was he wearing aftershave or did he have BO? the feel of his skin, the tone of his voice, his accent – *everything*."

"Well, the first thing I can definitely tell you is that it wasn't a *him*."

Andy screwed up his face. "How d'ya mean?"

Natalie sat bolt upright. "How do you think I mean? The person who grabbed hold of me in that field this afternoon and whispered a warning in my ear was, without a doubt, a woman."

Chapter 36

Sharon Moffett listened to the de-briefing with her arms folded over her ample bosom. Somehow, this news wasn't coming as a surprise.

Bevan was going over Natalie Flynn's witness statement with the team. "This woman is tall. Flynn reckoned that her mouth was level with the top of her head. The woman had to bend down to whisper in Flynn's ear."

"But Flynn is quite small, isn't she?" Andy added.

"About 5'3", I'd say," Sharon offered.

"Which makes our suspect 5'9" or over," Dani said, after making a few rudimentary measurements on the flip chart.

Dan Clifton raised his hand. "Do we still think the murders are being committed by a gang of people traffickers? This woman doesn't fit the profile."

Andy nodded in recognition of Clifton's logic. "Flynn wasn't sure of the woman's accent, but she's fairly certain it wasn't eastern European."

"She could be connected to the gang. This woman was only a messenger, remember," Dani put in.

Sharon stood up. "Yes, Ma'am, but the message sounded deeply personal. I wonder why she said Alan Flynn would be made to 'perform for the camera'." The DS puffed herself up. "I believe this woman was a *victim* of this gang. I don't think she was in any way involved in the operation of the business, or that she's trying to keep these men quiet. I believe she wants revenge."

A murmur of agreement rippled around the room.

Moffett appeared to be articulating what the rest of the team were all beginning to think.

Andy rubbed his chin. "If the woman who attacked Natalie was once filmed herself by those men, we need to go back to the footage retrieved from the crime scenes. I know we don't have all the material they produced, but we've got the older stuff."

"How would we even begin to identify her?" Dan looked incredulous.

Dani stepped forward. "This woman is tall. 5'9" has got to be an unusual height, hasn't it? Surely, we can at least narrow down our suspects from that information?"

Andy looked pained. "We're going to have to go back through all those tapes, folks. I'll get onto Vice and see if they can courier over the rest. This isn't going to be a pleasant task, but I think we've finally got ourselves a decent lead."

*

The embassy car drove Fergus Kelso out of the city, through the Longqing Valley and into Yanqing County. The landscape was impressive and populated by ancient villages dating back to the earliest ruling dynasties of China.

Fergus was too pre-occupied to enjoy the view from the tinted rear window of the Buick. He was lucky to have been provided with a driver at all. The young lawyer had practically begged Acomb to give him use of it for one last interview.

The Zhu property was accessed through an ornate security gate which was embedded within a stone barrier that would have given The Great Wall itself a run for its money. Inside, the outlook was less intimidating. A sweeping stone driveway weaved through immaculate gardens filled with the most glorious pink blossoms and cascading water features.

The MPV pulled up outside the entrance, with the driver coming around the side to slide open the door for his passenger. Fergus informed him to stay put until he returned.

The main house felt more like a hotel than a family home. Fergus entered a lobby which seemed designed to serve as a continuation of the garden. Giant potted plants dominated the floor space.

A lean man in a dark suit stepped forward to greet him. "Good afternoon, Mr Kelso. I am Zhu Li Jun. Now the head of the family."

Fergus knew this man was Deming's younger brother. "Thank you for agreeing to see me. I realise this is a difficult time for you."

Li Jun led his guest into a pleasant room which faced another pristine garden with the distant view of mountains. He took them to a set of chairs by the window.

"This house is very beautiful."

"The location is perfect. The family have been here for two generations now."

A woman in a smart uniform brought a tray of tea.

Li Jun leant forward as she poured the drinks. "You have not come here to exchange pleasantries. I hear you represent the legal team of my sister-in-law?"

"It's a little more complicated than that. My interest is in the appeal against Mrs Zhu's sentence, rather than the original trial or investigation."

"The two go hand-in-hand, I imagine."

Fergus found it difficult to read the man's mood. "Yes, that's inevitably true. We have found that the murder of Deming was more complicated than it first appeared. But we are running out of time to prove what really happened in that apartment on the evening he died."

Li Jun sipped his tea, replacing the cup carefully in its delicate saucer. "Did Charmian cause my brother's death, Mr Kelso?"

Fergus sighed. "I don't believe Deming died by her hand, but Mrs Zhu *was* responsible for bringing about his murder, yes. If your brother had never married her, he would still be alive."

"Then justice is being served."

"Don't you want to find out the truth?"

"The truth is not always welcome," Li Jun replied dryly. "If you have come here to provide us with information more distressing than the news we have already received, please re-consider."

Fergus did consider this. "Okay, then I'd be satisfied if you'd just answer me one question."

The man nodded.

"If your brother found out information about a crime, even if it implicated a person he loved very deeply, would he feel compelled to report it to the authorities?"

Li Jun didn't even blink before replying, "Yes, he would. Deming was a man of high principle. I often found myself on the wrong side of my brother's strict principles, so I should know best of all."

"Thank you. That's all I needed to hear from you. If you don't mind, I should like to finish this wonderful tea before I call the driver to take me back to the city."

"Of course, Mr Kelso. You are most welcome."

Chapter 37

The only Ciaran Maguire that Alice could find on the databases she'd scoured, who matched the correct age and background of the young man who'd lived in Blair Atholl until 1984, had died of a cardiac arrest at St James's Hospital, Dublin in 2008.

Karen must have been right when she suggested the Maguire boys had returned to Ireland after the bombing of the Maraig Barracks. Alice leant back against the cushions of her sofa. She and Fergus had discussed what she'd found out from Karen Wiley long into the previous night.

It had broken her heart to have to tell such a principled man as Fergus that his birth father was most likely a terrorist and a killer and Charmian very possibly the man's teenage accomplice in the murder of 19 innocent service personnel.

But the lawyer had taken it better than she'd expected. Fergus expressed relief that he'd been adopted and brought up by such decent people. There was no reason why the sins of the father should be visited upon the children. He was a completely different person to them.

The detail they couldn't fathom, however, was how this terrible crime from 33 years ago had led to Deming's murder in a sealed apartment in Beijing in the present day.

Alice had no doubt that Morgan Schrager's investigator found out a similar story to the one she'd uncovered. This information he passed onto his friend and soon-to-be business partner, Deming, whom he believed should know the truth about his wife.

Deming decided to investigate for himself, discovering that not only had his wife given birth to a child he knew nothing about, but she'd passed information to IRA operatives that had resulted in a heinous act of terrorism.

Fergus was now convinced that Deming confronted Charmian with what he'd found out about her past, possibly during their holiday. The young lawyer was finally being forced to concede that the woman had been lying to him. It seemed likely that Deming tried to persuade her to turn herself into a police station upon their return to China and confess everything. Charmian probably agreed, simply waiting for them to be at home in their flat with her gun before ensuring Deming's silence forever.

Alice still wondered about the attempt on Fergus's life in their hotel room. It didn't make any sense if there was no one else involved in Deming's murder but Charmian. Fergus suggested it could simply have been the random burglary the local police believed it to be. But Alice wasn't persuaded that sort of coincidence would ever really happen.

Which left one other theory. Deming's investigations had alerted those responsible for the bombing of the barracks that someone was getting close to the truth. Blair Atholl was a small place, perhaps one of Deming's phone calls was to an old friend of Charmian's who also knew the Maguires and tipped one of them off.

Fergus had queried if this information would really have mattered to anyone any longer, except the families of the poor victims. Not after the Good Friday Agreement had released so many of those responsible for terrorist crimes anyway.

But Alice considered what this type of revelation might mean for a man who nobody knew had any previous connections to the IRA, let alone had once been instrumental in an act of terror. This might be a secret worth taking extreme measures to protect. She stared again at her computer screen. Ciaran Maguire was long dead.

She sat up straighter. What about the younger brother? The boy who had sat in the front seat of the delivery van, day-in-day-out, entering and leaving the barracks with ease. Was he not the most likely to have been the one to slip away from his task of loading boxes for a few minutes and, using the information given to them by Charmian, found dorm C and planted their deadly homemade device?

There had been no record of an Aiden Maguire of the correct age living in Northern Ireland or the Republic, nor any evidence of his death. Alice suddenly recalled what Karen had said. How the USA may have been another place the boys might have disappeared to. What if the Maguire boys had taken different paths after '84? One remained in Ireland, whilst the other fled to another continent altogether, to make a new life. That's exactly what Charmian did, after all.

Chapter 38

Sharon Moffett had decided to stay in a B&B in Glasgow for a few nights. The volume of material sent through from Vice meant they were putting in a lot of overtime. She didn't fancy the commute back and forth from her house in Haddington each day. The neighbour was feeding her cat.

She rubbed her eyes and sipped the strong coffee she'd made from a couple of sachets of instant on the refreshment tray. It gave her a brief surge of adrenaline to focus back on the images playing out on her laptop.

This particular element of the job she hated. The grainy home videos that the techies had digitally enhanced were exploitative and nasty. Many of the girls appeared underage and frightened. But none seemed unusually tall or strong – as the woman who overpowered Natalie Flynn must surely have been.

In fact, it looked to Sharon as if the girls in the pornos had been chosen specifically because they could be physically dominated by the men exploiting them. The DS was increasingly coming to the conclusion that their theory of Karla – as she still liked to think of her – being one of the sex workers, didn't hold water.

Sharon shut down the screen and closed her eyes. Her intention was to think, but sleep quickly crept up on the detective and within minutes she'd slumped back against the pillows, her breathing deep and heavy. But she woke again almost as quickly as a thought popped into her head.

The DS reached out to the bedside cabinet for her phone and swiftly dialled.

"Calder," came the gruff reply.

"Sorry to bother you at home. It's Sharon."

"Not a problem, I'm up to my eyes in the kind of degrading pornography that makes you physically sick. So, no, I don't mind an interruption."

"Me neither. I was just taking a break from it when an idea struck me."

"Oh aye?"

Sharon shuffled up higher against the headboard. "I don't know about you, but I've not seen a single girl in these videos who I'd describe as tall or well built. These poor wee things look as if a strong gust of wind would sweep them away."

"Aye, I've found the same. The younger and frailer they are, the easier to exploit."

"Exactly. But the woman we're looking for is the opposite of that. She had to be strong enough to bludgeon Ken Garfield with a heavy, professional light stand and dispose of Robbie Addison's body in the sea. She must be strong and physically fit. Which made me think we could be looking in the wrong place for her. Where would you find a tall, strong and extremely fit woman?"

Andy was on his feet now. "In the army."

"Exactly," Sharon replied.

*

It was late, but Dani had decided to join her colleagues back at the station. She was intrigued by Sharon Moffett's theory and wanted to know more.

Andy had summoned up the lists given to him by the 5th Scots Battalion. "I hadn't given much attention to the women," he said sheepishly. "I was looking for possible associates of Dalgleish, so my focus was on males of a similar age who'd served with him for a significant period of time. That only threw up Addison and Garfield. Then, we found out Flynn and Dunn were involved too. When we cracked the acronym, I thought that was it."

Dani nodded. "It was a perfectly natural assumption to make. We always need to find ways to narrow the search. Plus, there really don't seem to be many females mentioned here, particularly back in the 70s and 80s."

Sharon moved in closer to the screen. The amended lists had included all personnel, not just the military. She scanned through the names. A couple caught her eye. "Look, there were two female members of the nursing corps stationed at Girdwood in the 80s. Can we find out more about them?"

Andy jotted down the names. "I can contact Major Marks again in the morning and get him to dig out their service files."

"Great," Dani said. "In the meantime, let's do our own searches on these women." She glanced at her watch. "Between the three of us, we should be able to pretty much find out their life stories by breakfast."

Chapter 39

By dawn, the detectives had discounted one of the two names. This woman had left the army in '87 to get married. In the mid-nineties, she and her family moved to Perth, Western Australia. Her Facebook page showed pictures of the whole clan basking on a beach less than a week earlier.

Which left them with Keira Morrison. According to battalion records, she'd joined the nursing corps at just eighteen and was stationed within months at Girdwood in Belfast. She was there from 1983 to 86.

As soon as the sun rose, Andy was e-mailing the 5th Battalion headquarters. By 9am he'd received a response. He lifted his head from the computer screen. "I've had a message from Major Marks's secretary. She's compiling the records for us now and will scan them over within the hour."

"Great," Sharon replied distractedly. She was punching Keira's name into just about every database the detective could think of. The woman had no criminal record, that much she'd ascertained already. She'd grown up in Lanark and attended a local school there, leaving just after her Highers to take her nursing qualifications within the corps. Finally, a picture popped up on Sharon's screen. It was from one of the Lanark papers. Keira had been photographed receiving a medal for winning a regional swimming gala.

Sharon twisted round her laptop. "Look at this," she entreated her colleague.

Andy glanced up. "Is that her?"

"Yep," Sharon replied. "She's only a teenager in this photo, but see how tall and broad she already is."

Andy stared hard at the image. Keira was certainly a tall girl, with long, dark hair tied back in a band from her very attractive face. "She matches the description of the woman Natalie Flynn remembered from the campsite in France in 1989."

Sharon nodded. "I'm convinced this is our woman. She definitely knew Dalgleish. Perhaps, for a time, Keira was his girlfriend."

Andy stretched his arms above his head. "I'll make us all a coffee." He paced towards the cubby-hole kitchen, suddenly feeling the effects of their night without sleep. His head was starting to throb gently. As he waited for the kettle to boil, Andy watched the day shift begin to filter onto the floor, thinking how they'd need to bring the entire team up to speed.

By the time he returned to his workstation, after delivering a coffee to the boss and balancing a brimming mug in each hand as he meandered carefully across the serious crime floor, his inbox was flashing with a new message.

*

Captain Chen, of the Beijing police department, had a tolerant expression on his face. The Zhu Deming murder case file sat on the desk in front of him.

"I realise you're doing me a great favour here, Captain. I appreciate it." Fergus was genuine in his gratitude. The man was clearly being as helpful as possible within the limits of his rank.

"I'm sorry we weren't able to apprehend the thief who broke into your hotel room. I wouldn't like you to leave our city with a poor impression of our law enforcement."

"I won't, I assure you. But my main concern is with the case against Mrs Zhu. My investigator has uncovered new evidence back in Scotland. We have discovered a third party who may have wished Mr and Mrs Zhu harm."

Chen crinkled his brow. "That's as maybe, but the circumstances of the murder could not have been more clear-cut." He counted points off on his fingers. "Mrs Zhu's fingerprints were found on the weapon. She was the only person who was present in the apartment at the time Zhu Deming was shot. Neighbours heard a disagreement between the husband and wife not long before the fatal shot was fired. All Mr Zhu's family and friends deny the man was suicidal. He'd just signed the business deal of his career. The evidence was conclusive, sir."

Fergus sat back against the hard chair, running through the evidence again in his head. Abruptly, he edged forward once more. "But Charmian Zhu *wasn't* the only person in the apartment around the time of Deming's death."

Chen screwed up his face. "What do you mean?"

"The security manager was in the flat too. He even had a key card which gave him unfettered access." Fergus rubbed his head vigorously. "Just like the intruder who got into our hotel room – he had an accomplice on the staff who gave him a security key which opened our door."

Chen put his hand up. "Slow down, Mr Kelso. You are making a connection between these two crimes which I'm not sure has been proven."

Fergus's tone became more energised. "*Of course* they must be connected! I came here to China to prove Charmian's innocence. As soon as I started digging around and asking questions, someone made an attempt on my life. That's not a coincidence."

Chen calmly opened up the file and sifted

through the contents. "The security manager's name is Gao Bohai. He is 53 years old and originally from Shandong province. His interview transcript is here. We checked him out thoroughly. Gao had worked for the management company for 20 years. His record was clean."

"My friend, the policewoman from Scotland, she was suspicious about the rug on the floor of the apartment. It was made from a synthetic material which was out of place with the other furnishings belonging to the Zhus."

"We have the rug in our evidence department. The gun was found resting on it."

"Yes," Fergus was trying to keep the frustration out of his tone. "But it was the management company who insisted that Deming lay the rug on the wooden floor. Apparently, there'd been complaints about the noise of their footfalls on the parquet from the couple downstairs. Did anyone actually question this couple to find out if they really did complain?"

Chen was looking at Fergus as if he'd lost his mind. "Of course not. This issue was unrelated to the shooting of Mr Zhu."

"I'm not sure it was," the lawyer replied flatly. "Why would someone wish to place an object in another's private apartment?"

Chen shrugged his shoulders, his patience clearly running thin. "I've no idea, Mr Kelso."

"So they could insert a listening device into it. The management company wanted to know what Deming and Charmian were talking about in private."

"We found no such device in the rug."

"That's because Gao had plenty of time to remove it, after he had shot Deming and whilst Mrs Zhu was taking a shower. He then left the apartment, giving

Charmian time to discover her husband's body. He *returned* when she had retreated into her bedroom in shock. Making it appear that Mrs Zhu was the only person present when her husband was killed."

"How did Gao know where to find Mrs Zhu's gun? Or when it was safe for him to enter the flat and take Mr Zhu by surprise?"

"Gao had the run of the place. When the Zhus were at work he could easily have found where the gun was kept. The listening device would have told him when Charmian had gone into the suite to have her shower. Gao could have knocked on the door with any kind of pretext. Whilst Deming was distracted, Gao fetched the gun and shot him in the head. Perhaps he asked him to retrieve a piece of paperwork. Deming had no reason to fear the manager. He thought he was there to protect them. It was the same assumption we made."

Chen shook his head. "But *why* should the man do it? What motive would such an ordinary person as Gao Bohai have to murder a prominent businessman and frame his wife?"

Fergus sighed. "The security manager had no motive at all, except money. We are talking about a very powerful person behind all this, with the kind of money that can make anything happen, in any place, at any time. The man behind Zhu Deming's murder paid a great deal of money to orchestrate the crime. More than we can probably dream of. It was perfectly planned and executed."

Captain Chen gave a half smile and waggled his finger at Fergus. "I thought for a while that the theory you were proposing was serious. But this is just a story, is it not? To inject an element of doubt so that your citizen will be spared the firing squad?" The policeman shuffled the notes back into the file and closed it decisively. "Because this theory cannot be proved by evidence. It is purely a flight of fancy."

Fergus nodded sadly. "Yes, I realise that. It's far too late to prove any of this. He's undoubtedly going to get away with it, all over again."

Chapter 40

It struck Andy as ironic that they were back where the case had first begun. Instead of Alice, it was Sharon in the seat beside him as they pulled up at the semi-detached property in Newton Mearns. The broken blinds were still lowered in front of the living room window.

"Will we need back-up?" Sharon suddenly asked, as her colleague turned off the engine.

They'd left the station in a hurry. Andy was just reading through Keira Morrison's service record, sent through from the 5th Scots Regiment headquarters, when Sharon's DVLA search listed the last known address for the woman as the house in Newton Mearns owned by Len Dalgleish.

"I don't think so. We've no idea if she's staying here. It would be risky if she was, as we've already raided the place."

"Or particularly clever," Sharon replied levelly. "We've not been back here since Vice cleared it out and Dalgleish has been on remand."

"True enough." Andy climbed out of the car and approached the house. "There's only one way to find out."

Sharon hammered on the front door whilst Andy walked down the side passage, weaving around the set of wheelie bins, which he noted had recently been filled with black bags.

As Sharon began calling through the letterbox, Andy heard the screech of an old patio door being slid open. He hovered at the end of the passageway until spotting a figure making a dash for it across the back lawn.

Calder set off in pursuit. He had to admit she was fast. He wasn't as fit as he'd been during his recuperation, when he was working out every day. The DS made a mental note to get himself back into shape.

The fence that ran along the rear of the plot held her up. She had to pause for a moment to get a grip on the ledge at the top. Andy took the opportunity to dive for her legs, tugging the woman to the hard ground with a thud.

Keira wriggled violently, kicking with both feet and trying to catch Andy in the groin. But the detective's weight was too much for her. And when he noticed she wasn't wearing any shoes, Andy dragged her arms behind her back and planted himself squarely on the woman's thighs, reasonably confidently that she wouldn't be getting away anytime soon.

Sharon puffed down the garden to join him, a sweaty sheen on her upper lip. "I've called for back-up," she offered with a grin.

Andy proceeded to read Keira her rights, thinking that the super-fit Alice Mann did actually have some characteristics in her favour after all.

*

Dani was observing the interview from the media suite. This was very much Calder and Moffett's collar. She was happy to allow them to take on the suspect now she'd been apprehended.

Keira Morrison was fifty-two years old, but obviously kept herself in good shape. Her hair remained dark and wavy, but she wore it now in a bob to her shoulders. The woman's long legs were folded up beneath the table, but her strong upper body was visible for all to see. She had only the scrawny duty solicitor to one side and Keira's dominating presence made him look small and insignificant.

Sharon broke the silence. "For the benefit of the tape, can you confirm that you are Keira Jane Morrison, currently residing at 22 Govan Street, Newton Mearns?"

Keira released a non-comital grunt.

"We need a clear answer for the recording, Miss Morrison."

"Yes."

"And you are the girlfriend of Leonard Dalgleish, now on remand pending charges of producing and distributing extreme pornographic material."

"That's got nothing to do with me," she hissed.

"But you are his girlfriend?" Sharon persisted.

"Yes, on and off."

"What does that mean?"

"We were together for a long time. Then we split up, in the early nineties. We got back together again a few years back."

Andy skimmed through his notes. "You met Dalgleish when you were stationed together at the Girdwood army barracks in Belfast, between 1983 and '86. Is that correct? You were a nurse there?"

Keira nodded. "I always wanted to join the army, but my old man wouldn't have it. He said it was no job for a girl. So, my only way in was through nursing."

"When did you and Dalgleish become an item?"

She examined her fingernails. "Len got injured policing a march in the city. He got a flying bottle to the temple. He came into the infirmary and I treated him. It started then, a few months after I'd arrived. I was very young and he seemed like a nice guy."

"But he wasn't?" Sharon enquired innocently.

Keira glanced up. "It was complicated. Life was tough for us back then. Len's always done what he had to in order to make a living for himself. He didn't enjoy it."

"Did you know he was making pornographic films?" Andy leant forward. "You must have done. There was a studio in your front room for heaven's sake!"

Keira sighed heavily. "Of course I did. But I made sure the girls were okay. Len only did it for the money. He had debts to pay off. We made sure the girls weren't mistreated."

Sharon tried to keep the expression of disgust from her face. "According to your service records, you were transferred to the British base at Bielefeld, Germany in September 1986. How did this affect your relationship?"

"Len wanted to leave the army, he'd had enough by then. He hated it, in truth. But was worried about how to make ends meet without the steady wage. I still wanted to play my part. I was in western Germany for three years. Len came out and visited me. But I realised I missed him."

"So, you applied for a discharge from the army which was granted in May 1989," Andy continued. "Loverboy Len even took the ferry to Calais and drove to Bielefeld, in the North Rhine Westphalia, in a hired van to pick you up and bring you back with all your stuff."

Keira looked sharply at the detective. "How the hell did you know that?"

"You stopped on the way home to meet Alan Flynn and his family at a campsite in Normandy. Young Natalie remembered you – a tall, beautiful woman with dark hair and too much make-up."

Keira's body flinched at the mention of Natalie

Flynn.

"This was the summer that the men decided on how they were going to make their money outside of the army. Alan and Len must have been discussing it that very day, sitting out on camping chairs in the sunshine, beers in their hands."

"I had nothing to do with it," Keira spat. "I didn't know what those bastards were planning. Of course, Janet was totally clueless as well, stupid cow. She had no idea what her sleazy husband was up to. Janet believes and says what Alan wants her to. Her head is an empty shell."

"That's not far from the truth," Sharon added dryly.

Andy narrowed his eyes. "But what did it have to do with you? Why did you come to hate them so much? Enough to want them all dead?"

Keira folded her arms across her chest, her mouth fixed in a grim line. "No, comment," she said.

Chapter 41

Dan Clifton burst through the door of the media suite.

Bevan swung around in her chair, her expression steely. "What the hell's the matter with you, Clifton? Can't you bloody well knock?"

"There's something you need to see, Ma'am. Straight away!"

Sharon and Andy were just returning from the interview room when they spotted the DCI beckoning them over.

"Dan has unearthed some new evidence," she said with some excitement. "I'll let him explain."

Andy and Sharon each pulled up a chair.

"Well, it wasn't really down to me," Dan explained. "The DI at Highlands and Islands called, he wanted to speak to Andy, but I said he was interviewing, so he sent me the contents of the tape instead."

"What tape?" Andy tried to keep his voice level.

"Addison's niece travelled over to the farmhouse on Mull. After the division tracked her down and took a sample of her DNA to compare with her uncle's remains, she was informed by his solicitors that she'd inherited the property on Mull. There were no other surviving relatives."

Andy resisted the urge to grab the young DC by the scruff of his neck to shake the information out of him faster. "What did she find?"

"The niece is clearing the entire place out, with the intention of selling up. She found a loose floorboard in the airing cupboard. Apparently, she was checking the condition of the old waterpipes." Dan glanced at Andy, saw his eye was twitching with anger, so decided to speed things up. "She found a box hidden under there. Inside was an old-fashioned video tape. She knew what dodgy stuff her uncle had been involved in, so she handed it straight in to the police station at Tobermory, who passed it on to Oban. The DI up there had it converted into digital format." He took a breath. "I've just watched it. I think you better had too."

*

Sharon was fighting hard to resist the urge to put her hands up to cover her face. The officers were crammed into DCI Bevan's office, watching the amateur film on her laptop.

The backdrop to the action was the barn at Addison's farm on Mull. The barn itself looked little different than it did when Garfield's body was discovered there a few weeks previously. But the ages of the participants suggested it was recorded at least twenty years earlier than that.

A young woman was tied naked to the middle of the iron framed beds. Sharon could quite clearly see that it was Keira Morrison. Surrounding her were Robert Addison, Kenneth Garfield, Alan Flynn and Angus Dunn. These men went on to perform acts upon Keira that made Sharon's stomach churn.

The video lasted for about an hour. At the end of it, the detectives sat in silence for several moments.

It was Dani who broke the tension. "There's our motive," she said quietly. "If someone had done that to me, I'd want to put them six feet under."

Andy wiped his hands down his trousers. "This happened a long time ago. Why is Keira only taking revenge now?"

Sharon stood up. "Let's bring this nasty little tape with us into the interview room and ask her."

*

Andy had no intention of showing Keira Morrison the full tape. He wasn't a complete bastard. He only had the opening scene freeze-framed and displayed on his laptop. He spun it around to face their interviewee and observed her reaction.

The woman's composure crumpled. Her lips trembled and tears escaped onto her pale cheeks.

"What is this, DS Calder?" The duty solicitor asked sternly. "My client hasn't been warned about any new pieces of evidence."

"It's only just come into our possession. We simply need to ask Keira a few questions about it."

The woman convulsed with sobs. "I didn't know there were any copies left," she wailed.

"Addison kept one," Andy explained.

Sharon made sure her tone was gentle. "Keira, why don't you tell us about what happened. Any jury in the country would have sympathy for you after watching that tape. If you cooperate with us, you might even serve a shorter sentence than Dalgleish will."

The woman wiped her face with the back of her hand. "Really?"

"Or, if you continue to stone wall us, this evidence will be completely damning, added to Natalie Flynn's testimony, pertaining to the woman who accosted her and promised to murder her dad, I can see you dying in jail." Andy's voice was menacing.

The tears were threatening to fall again.

Sharon intervened, "all you need to do is talk to me, Keira. I want to try and help you. I can see you were a victim in all this."

The woman nodded. "I am. I wanted nothing to do with Addison's business scheme. When Len told me about it, I was disgusted. I told him not to get involved. But Len worked on me, persuaded me that it wasn't much worse than the top shelf mags they used to sell in the corner shops, or page three of The Sun." She lifted her head, "and it wasn't too bad at first. Addison had some local girls posing with their tops off for a few bob. Len helped to sell the pictures. The money was really good."

"When did things start to change?"

Keira cleared her throat. "Ken Garfield got a job for Murray's Haulage. He must have had some unsavoury contacts on the continent because by the early nineties, he was smuggling girls into the country in the back of his truck. These girls were taken over to Addison's farm on Mull. Then the videos got nastier."

"Why didn't you contact the police."

Her face clouded with sadness. "Because Len was involved up to his eyeballs. He was making films in his front room – nothing as bad as Addison's stuff – and sending them up to Mull for distribution."

Sharon took a breath. "When did they make the film of you?"

Keira dropped her vision to the table top. "Len had some tapes to deliver to Addison. He usually took them himself." She gave a hollow laugh. "But on this occasion, he had a meeting at work. I had a few days free, so he asked me to take them instead. Len had no idea what was going to happen. I reckon Len had complained to Addison about how I didn't like what was going on. So, the rest of them decided to teach me a lesson – or keep me quiet, one or the other."

"Dalgleish definitely wasn't there when the assault on you occurred?" Andy clarified.

"No, of course not. He was my partner, he wouldn't have allowed them to do it." The tears were dripping down her cheeks once more. "I arrived on the late boat. Ken came and picked me up in the van. He was all jokes and smiles. We got to the farm and I gave Addison the tapes from Len. Then the atmosphere changed. I didn't understand why they were all there. Every single one of the men I'd first met at Girdwood ten years earlier, except Len. Addison started to tell me he'd always fancied me, especially when I was in my nurse's uniform, just eighteen." She swallowed back a sob. "I'm a strong woman, I've always taken care of myself, but I was no match for the four of them. I thought they were going to kill me, to be honest. I was sort of aware they were filming it, but I didn't really consider that until later. After they were through, Addison dragged me out into the woods and left me there overnight. I was naked and bleeding. I'm amazed I survived. But I did. In the early hours, I sneaked back in. The bastards were sleeping like babies. I found some clothes and hitch-hiked to the ferry port."

"Did you tell Dalgleish?" Sharon asked.

"Not straight away. I took some money from Addison's wallet before I left. I used it to reach a friend's house in Lanark. I stayed there for a while. I couldn't face Len. I blamed him, you see."

"I can imagine that. He was the man who sent you there, got you involved with those men in the first place."

Keira shook her head sadly. "That's when we split up. He didn't understand why. Len was really upset. He loved me. But after a couple of years had passed,

I realise it wasn't his fault. It was those evil men, not him."

"You returned to Dalgleish?"

"I turned up on his doorstep three years after I'd left for Mull. I told him everything that had happened in that barn at the farmhouse. Len was angry, completely incensed with rage. But I told him to hold it back. He was too closely involved. If their business got exposed, then he would go to prison too, me as well probably." She shuddered. "But Len insisted on one thing. He wanted any tapes of the rape destroyed. He couldn't bear to think of Addison selling them on the open market. He called Robbie up at the farm and told him to get rid of any tape that existed. He informed him plainly that it didn't matter if we all rotted in prison, if he ever saw a copy of the tape in circulation, he'd go straight to the police."

"It seems like he just kept the one copy, for insurance perhaps."

Keira glanced briefly at the image on Calder's laptop screen. "Can you switch that off? I can't stand to see it."

Andy placed his hands flat on the table between them. "I'll do you a deal. You tell us exactly how you killed Addison, Garfield and Dunn. Then I'll switch that thing off and you'll never have to set eyes on its contents again."

Chapter 42

Sharon felt her lip curling up into a snarl when she caught sight of Alan Flynn exiting the door of his tiny flat.

She strode towards him with cuffs at the ready. His expression was one of surprise as the DS swept his arm behind his back and read him his rights.

"Alan Flynn, I'm arresting you for the aggravated rape of Keira Morrison on the 15th May, 1993. You do not have to say anything. But it may harm your defence if you do not mention when questioned something you later rely on in court. Anything you do say may be taken in evidence."

Janet Flynn dashed out of the door, her slippers still on and her dressing gown flapping open to reveal a flannelette nightie. "What's happening, Alan? Why is she arresting you? What did she say about a *rape*?"

Flynn's angry eyes flashed at Sharon. "If you're arresting *me*, what about that crazy bitch? She clearly murdered Robbie and Ken! It's her you need to be locking up!"

Sharon ignored him, pulling the cuffs sharply, until she made the man beside her wince in pain.

*

DCI Bevan had called the team into the briefing room. There was a palpable atmosphere of exhilaration.

Dani stepped forward. "I'll be visiting DCS Douglas this afternoon at home to provide him with an update. Currently, we have Keira Morrison in custody." She glanced at her watch. "Right about now, she'll be being charged with the murders of Ken Garfield, Robert Addison and Angus Dunn, in addition to the assault on Natalie Flynn. We have also arrested Alan Flynn for the rape of Morrison in 1993. Whichever way you look at it, this is one hell of a result."

A ripple of applause went around the room.

"Did Morrison confess?" Dan asked.

Andy stepped forward. "Yes, she gave a full account of the murders in interview. It was the arrest of Dalgleish which triggered her revenge. It was purely by chance that Alice and I stumbled upon his homemade porno studio. Once her boyfriend was on remand, Keira saw no further reason not to act. The assault had eaten her up inside. She'd dreamt of being able to get even with her rapists."

"Did Dalgleish know about what she had planned?" Dan persisted.

"Keira claims he had no idea. But I don't believe that's true. We interviewed him twice. Not once did he mention his girlfriend's existence. He must have known she was the one killing off his associates. He understood the strong motive she had."

"Keira turned up at the farmhouse on Mull," Sharon continued. "The reason she gave to Addison was that she wanted to discuss how to get Dalgleish out of prison. Garfield turned up too, worried that Len's arrest was going to implicate them all. Keira waited until the men were alone before she bludgeoned them both with the base of a light stand. She left Garfield's body where it was. But drove Addison's remains to a lonely clifftop and rolled his body over the edge. Her hope was that his disappearance would lead us to think Addison killed Garfield."

"Which we nearly did," Andy added.

"Keira knew her prints would be in the farmhouse, but she'd no criminal record and if Dalgleish could be trusted not to talk, we wouldn't be taking her prints for analysis. Besides, she knew there would be hundreds of other prints in that barn, from all the girls that had been brought there over the years. There was no reason to single her out."

"By comparison," Andy supplied. "The murder of Angus Dunn was easy. His restaurant had featured on the TV and in the national press. Keira just had to watch the place from the rear to pick up on Dunn's habit of having a post service fag every evening. She parked at the end of the alleyway, dressed in black, and waited with a kitchen knife for Dunn to walk into her trap."

Dani ran a hand through her hair. "Although the murders were cleverly executed, it was almost as if Keira was just waiting to be caught. She was still living at Dalgleish's place all this time, wasn't she?"

"Yes, Ma'am," Sharon replied. "She was at work when we raided the place and waited for the police presence to peter out before she returned. But I'm not sure Keira really had a plan for when she'd completed her killing spree. I believe her only aim was to be free to punish her rapists. When she realised Alan Flynn was getting police protection, she resorted to the assault on Natalie. It smacked of desperation. I don't think Keira cared much for self-preservation."

"And it was the reason we found her," Dani added with emphasis. "It was Natalie's description of the woman who accosted her that made Sharon think she was ex-military."

Andy sighed heavily. "That tape Keira was so keen to have destroyed might just be what saves her. I reckon when the jury see it, they'll side with Keira over her victims. I can't see her serving a full life sentence."

"Well," Dani said philosophically. "That isn't our concern. We've played our part as best we can." She stepped forward and shook Andy and Sharon each by the hand. "This was fantastic investigative work, for which I will commend you both to the DCC." She addressed the female officer, "I don't suppose you fancy hanging around in Glasgow for a little while longer?"

Sharon shrugged her shoulders and chuckled. "I'll certainly think about it, Ma'am."

Chapter 43

As she walked through the arrivals gate, Alice tried to play it cool. But as soon as Fergus emerged from the bustling crowd and moved towards her, the detective dropped her case and fell into his arms.

"You didn't have to come back," he murmured into her shoulder. "But I'm bloody glad you did."

She laughed. "I had to see it through to the end."

He nodded solemnly. They both knew what that meant. The end was Charmian Zhu's execution, scheduled for the following day.

They found a nearby hotel with a decent looking bar and settled into a bay seat. Alice pulled her briefcase onto her lap and delved inside. She pulled out a copy of the Washington Post and handed it to her companion. "Take a look at page two."

Fergus flicked over to a double-page spread featuring the businessman-cum politician, Paul Aiden Maguire, with a large glossy photograph to accompany it. The man was now in his late forties, a bit portly, but still strikingly handsome and with a full head of thick, dark hair.

"Christ, there's quite a resemblance." Fergus stared at the picture until a waitress brought their drinks. He glanced up at Alice. "You were the one who questioned the witnesses. Do you think he is my father?"

Alice shook her head. "I'm fairly sure it was the older brother, Ciaran. He stayed in Ireland after fleeing Scotland. But Aiden headed to the United States, where republicanism wasn't such a dirty word. He arrived in New York with nothing, switched his names around, became known as Paul and proceeded to build up a huge distribution business that's made him a billionaire."

Fergus whistled. "Now he's the Democratic Governor of East Hampshire. A man known for his ardent support for greater gun controls."

"The kind of person who wouldn't want a past association with terrorist violence to come out into the open." Alice sipped her club soda.

Fergus shook his head. "Do you truly believe that Maguire organised Deming's shooting, framing Charmian in the process?"

Alice nodded. "Actually, I do. When someone tipped Paul Maguire off that Deming was investigating Charmian's role in the barracks bombing, he'd probably forgotten his brother's teenage girlfriend ever existed. Now he had a problem. If Deming persuaded his wife to confess to her part in the atrocity, Maguire's whole political empire would come tumbling down."

"But Beijing seems so far away from East Hampshire, USA."

"The world is a small place for these people. Money can buy you connections and influence anywhere."

"I get that, but I can't shake the feeling that maybe Charmian killed him herself. She was responsible for the deaths of nineteen young men, some not more than boys. What did one more murder matter to protect her secret?"

Alice shrugged, nestling back into the soft velvet of the upholstered bench. "I can't be certain which of us is correct. The neighbours closest to the apartment heard Charmian and Deming arguing that night. I think it was Deming trying to persuade his wife to come clean. Either the security manager heard the exchange on the listening device and decided it was time to act, or Charmian realised her husband wasn't going to give up. She needed to get rid of him before he went to the police with what he knew."

Fergus leant forward and placed a kiss on her lips. "I don't want to think about it any more today. Let me call a cab and take you back to my hotel room. We've got some lost time to make up for."

Alice smiled, slipping her arm through the strap of her bag. "Just lead the way."

Chapter 44

As the sunlight filtered past the bars of the tiny window, high up on her cell wall, Charmian Zhu was informed through the hatch that she had a visitor.

Despite her weakened state, depleted by a diet she could barely stomach and the strain of her incarceration, the prisoner leapt to her feet and dressed quickly.

She didn't know why, but Charmian half-hoped it was the young lawyer with the dark hair. Not necessarily to tell her that the appeal had been granted – she wasn't naïve enough to believe that was possible, but simply to talk to her, maybe hold her hand before the end.

When the guards led her into a small chapel, off one of the main corridors of the prison, which she'd not previously known existed, her hopes were dashed.

A small, bald man in a cassock was standing in front of a mounted crucifix atop a make-shift Altar table. It was many years since Charmian had chosen to be in a place such as this.

The man stepped forward and smiled. He took her limp hands in his. "Charmian, my child. Father Dalry sent me. I'm going to be with you until the final moment. You won't be alone, God will be walking with you."

Charmian sighed. How had that buffoon Dalry reached her out here? She thought she'd escaped those people decades before. It must have been her husband's meddling into her past that rattled the old priest's cage. "I didn't send for you, Father. Your assistance will not be needed."

He crinkled his brow with concern. "Don't turn your back on God at this crucial moment, Charmian. Father Dalry is concerned for your soul. I've travelled to your side to hear your confession and read you the last rites. It's imperative that you make peace before it is too late."

Charmian withdrew her hands from his soft grip. "Then you've had a wasted trip, Father. My conscience is clear. I haven't a single sin to confess to."

The old priest nodded solemnly, gazing into her mad, empty eyes. He muttered a prayer under his breath anyway and allowed the guards to take lead her out.

Chapter 45

James couldn't remember the last time they'd read the Sunday papers together in bed. He sipped his espresso with a self-satisfied expression on his face.

"Stop being smug," Dani muttered, as she scanned through the news section of the Herald, sitting up beside him.

He chuckled. "I'm not being *smug*, I'm simply feeling at peace with my existence."

Dani reached across and flicked his dressing gown cord at his head. "Now you're being pretentious too."

"Watch it! I'll spill my coffee on your ivory duvet cover."

Dani stopped flicking and picked the paper back up. "Good point."

James peered over her shoulder. "They found him guilty then?"

"Who?" Dani was temporarily confused, particularly with the number of prisoners they had awaiting trial from the Dalgleish case.

"The schoolboy accused of manslaughter," he said flatly. "The one we argued about."

"Oh yes." Dani read the news piece with interest. The boy, now 17 years old, had been found guilty of causing the death of his schoolmate due to reckless behaviour during the lunch break. The editorial was full of strong opinions on the issue, as one might expect.

"Wasn't Rhodri assisting the defence on that one? He'll be disappointed with the result."

"I'm not so sure. Their argument was going to be diminished responsibility due to a birth defect, causing brain damage. But I sensed Rhodri wasn't terribly convinced himself."

"That's not like him. The boy must have been an absolute monster." James placed his empty cup on the bedside table and rolled on top of her, crinkling the paper beneath his chest.

"I was reading that."

James kissed her lips and neck. "Oh dear, what a shame."

Dani giggled. "I thought you were on his side? The rugby-playing bully-boy."

James glanced up. "I had a re-think. Imagine if some young thug wrestled our son to the ground and knocked him unconscious. We'd want the full force of the law brought to bear."

Dani glanced about the room exaggeratedly. "Have I missed something? I don't believe we actually have a son." She grinned.

"It's, you know, *hypothetical*."

Dani touched his cheek. "Yes, I do know. I'm only teasing."

James's expression became more serious. "But I thought that what with Alice back in the department and Sharon becoming a more permanent feature, we might just think a bit more about this *hypothetical* son – or *daughter*, of course."

"Oh, okay." Dani was taken aback.

"Sorry, I'm moving a bit too fast, especially after everything that's happened." James's eyes widened, becoming almost puppy-like. "It's just that what with Howell's revelation and all this business with the FAS, it struck me that we'd do so much better a job."

He laughed. "I'm really not putting this very well, am I?"

Dani looked thoughtful. "Actually, you're not doing badly. The thought did cross my mind too."

James moved his face closer to hers, nuzzling her cheek. "Fine. Then we'll add it to the agenda?"

"Yes," she replied. "I think I'm okay with that."

If you enjoyed this novel, please take a few moments to write a brief review. Reviews really help to introduce new readers to my books and this allows me to keep on writing.

Many thanks,

Katherine.

If you would like to find out more about my books and read my reviews and articles then please visit my blog, TheRetroReview at:

www.KatherinePathak.wordpress.com

To find out about new releases and special offers follow me on Twitter:

@KatherinePathak

Most of all, thanks for reading!

Made in the USA
San Bernardino, CA
23 August 2018